Summer turns into a n_____ _____ _____
when his brother Ke_____ _____ _____.
Kevin, whom Jim idoli___ ___ _____ drastically during his year away. He has become a person full of
doubts, with urgent needs—one of which is drugs.

In Jim's revealing journal, which is the substance of
this moving book, we share the experience of that terrible summer—the LSD and marijuana, the hippies, the
disillusionment, the helpless confusion and fear. It is all
recorded frankly, to the final horror of Kevin's freak-
ing out and the shaky beginnings of his redemption.

MAIA WOJCIECHOWSKA is the author of the Newbery-
Award-winning *Shadow of a Bull*. Among her other
books for young people are *A Kingdom In a Horse*,
The Hollywood Kid and *A Single Light*.

THE LAUREL-LEAF LIBRARY brings together under a single
imprint outstanding works of fiction and nonfiction
particularly suitable for young adult readers, both in
and out of the classroom. This series is under the editor-
ship of M. Jerry Weiss, Distinguished Professor of
Communications, Jersey City State College, and
Charles Reasoner, Associate Professor, Elementary
Education, New York University.

TUNED OUT

OUT

A NOVEL BY

Maia Wojciechowska

Published by
Dell Publishing Co., Inc.
750 Third Avenue, New York, N. Y. 10017
Copyright © 1968 by Maia Wojciechowska
Reprinted by arrangement with Harper & Row, Publishers,
Incorporated, 49 East 33rd Street, New York, N. Y. 10016
to whom inquiries should be addressed
Laurel-Leaf Library ® TM 766734, Dell Publishing Co., Inc.
Printed in the United States of America
First Laurel printing—September, 1969
Second Laurel printing—December, 1969
Third Laurel printing—May, 1970
Fourth Laurel printing—August, 1970
Fifth Laurel printing—September, 1970

All the characters and situations in this
novel are fictitious, but names of the
author's friends have been used with their
consent.

for Nick, Stevie, Gigs, and Ronnie
because for each the summer of 1967 was a time of learning

"I see the boys of summer in their ruin . . ."
—Dylan Thomas

TUNED
OUT

AUTHOR'S NOTE

In Tuned Out *I have written of the summer of
1967. In many ways it was the summer of the
"hippies." In New York's East Village it came to
an end with the fall, and with the murder of two
young people. The summer of 1968 will not be
the same. Other summers will come and go but
the summer of 1967 will not resemble them. The
"drug scene" is no longer centralized in New York
or San Francisco; it has already spread from colleges and cities to high schools in the suburbs. It
will probably affect, before it too disappears,
every young person in the country. But we shall
all survive that as we have survived other dis-
asters.*

*Maia Wojciechowska
Oakland, N.J., March, 1968*

1967

One day I ought to find out how it is with other kids. I don't think I'm abnormal or anything for sixteen, but I don't think that there are many guys my age who are still crazy about their older brothers. They might actually love them, but I just don't think they are crazy about them. That's something you should outgrow, I guess, but I haven't. I've never made a big-deal secret out of it. As a small kid I used to get a lot of ribbing about it, and later on I had to fight a lot of guys who made fun of it. But now I just don't talk about it to anyone. It's not that I'm ashamed of it or anything like that, but how do you explain that Kevin is not just a brother to me? Besides being the greatest guy I know, he's someone I've got to have. I mean it's very important to me to have him.

Anyway he's been away at college in Chicago. He was going to come home for Thanksgiving, then for Christmas, then for spring vacation. But he didn't. And finally, today, he's actually coming back!

The kids I run around with wouldn't understand that I want to spend the summer with him. So I just told them that I won't be seeing them, that I'll be mostly away. I didn't want to go into details. I mean I didn't really want to tell them the truth, and the truth is that

I'd rather be with Kevin than with them. And that goes for any time.

Before he left he promised to write me. But all I got were a couple of letters, not really letters, just sort of scribbles I could barely make out. I kept writing him the first couple of months practically every day, and then he wrote me that I shouldn't be knocking myself out writing him so much. He said he didn't even have time to read my letters, and that I should keep a sort of a notebook instead. If anything really exciting happened, I should put it down and he'd read it when he got home. But nothing exciting is happening to me when he's away. Mostly I just goof with the other guys and some girls who hang around the Wigwam, which is a place we have where we just sit around and drink Cokes. Anyway I got not one but two lousy notebooks, and they've been just lying around gathering dust. But now that he's coming home I intend to write in one. There is only a three-year difference between us, but it might as well be a hundred. I'm that dumb and he's that bright. He really is. He knows everything. I mean you can ask him a question about anything at all and he'll tell you. And not in some crummy way, but sort of sharing his knowledge, if you know what I mean. No kidding, I'm so impressed with Kevin I had the idea once that when he grew up I could hang around him being his Boswell, for God's sakes. When I told him this, he said: "What the hell are you talking about, being my Boswell?"

"Sure," I said. "You'll be leading this fantastic life and I'll just hang around putting everything you say and do down on paper."

"What for, what for?" he yelled, and I could see he was getting real steamed up. "What do you mean putting everything down on paper? Nobody goes around doing a crazy thing like that!"

"Boswell did!" I said. "All he was doing was keeping score of the excitement . . ."

But I still think it's a great idea, and I figure he'll get used to it in time. So writing in this notebook is sort of a practice run for me.

At Christmas, when he didn't come home, I was really hurt. He didn't even send me a present or anything, just a lousy card. So what I did was I sent him all the money I had in my savings account. That was over three hundred dollars. And I didn't tell him the truth about where it came from, I wrote him that it was half of my winnings playing bingo. Bingo, for God's sakes! I wouldn't be caught dead playing that game. But he must have believed it because he never tried to send it back to me or anything. Anyway he did sort of thank me, but he certainly didn't make a big deal out of it and it was all the money I had. But what I really was hurt about was that he didn't have time to even read my letters. I figure if a guy has time to eat he's got time to read crummy letters from his own brother.

But then I forgave him. I mean he must have been very busy with his school work and everything. He was an honors student in high school but college isn't the same. You always hear how, in the first year, you go out of your mind just finding the right classrooms and things. So I stopped bugging him, except about once a month, just to let him know that I was still alive.

I really shouldn't start writing today, not until he actually gets here, but there is nothing to do and I don't feel like going to the Wigwam to see the kids. I mean all I can think about is seeing Kevin and that's what I'd talk about and they wouldn't understand. The kids I goof around with are a pretty great bunch but there isn't one special friend among them. They're just all my friends.

Anyway, Kevin will be here at four o'clock and it's two thirty already. We'll be leaving soon for the airport. Dad took the afternoon off from his job just for that. Mom has been fussing in Kevin's room all morning long and I poked around his things until she chased me out. Now I can hear dad beginning to pace up and down in the living room, muttering to himself. He does that whenever he is nervous or impatient. And he must be both. We all are.

I don't really know what mom and dad think of Kevin, except I know they are proud of him. More than that, they actually respect him. That seems strange in a way because I've never known a parent who respects one of his kids. But it's not really that strange with Kevin. You owe him that; you owe him respect. Maybe that came first. Maybe they started respecting him first, and then he got to be the unusual kid he is. Or maybe he was an unusual kid first, and they respected him for that.

The thing about Kevin is that he isn't like the other kids I know. I mean he isn't that offbeat or anything, and he goofs around a lot like everybody else, but he is *important*. For one thing he never says ordinary, cruddy things. When he speaks he almost always says something really brilliant. All the other guys I know, and that certainly goes double for the girls, they try to be brilliant, and they can't make it. Kevin doesn't have to try. Most of the time, listening to him, I feel that I am being handed the whole truth about the world, and about life, and about everything. I mean I'm really influenced by him. In everything.

It's late, and we still haven't gone to meet Kevin. We were just about to pile into the Chevy when this Western Union guy comes riding up on his bike. He's an ancient guy and I really flip over these oldsters. I mean it really gets me seeing some skinny old guy, weak with age, making a living for himself. I almost always imagine a whole bunch of things about them, the way they live, in real god-awful, smelly rooms, with mean landladies, and about what kind of crap they have for breakfast, like corn flakes out of the box, without even milk or anything.

Well, this guy is pumping the bike so hard I can see his skinny old hairy legs and he stops in front of our house. Mom's face goes real white, like every time there is a telegram, and she just stands there, like petrified, with her hand on the car door. Dad makes a big, loud show of it, saying that it's probably from his office, but he's nervous too. He takes a hell of a long time finding a quarter for the old guy who is just standing there sort of resting and looking goofy and sad. I look at mom again and I know she is praying by now. She really hates telegrams worse than anything else in the world. Then dad finally reads the message:

MISSED THE PLANE. ARRIVING 4 A.M. WILL TAKE CAB HOME. KEVIN.

So we all pile back into the house. Mom and dad are saying that they'll pick him up anyway.

"How about me?" I ask them.

"You can come too," mom says and then she adds: "that is, if you get to bed by eight."

That really makes me furious. I go back to my room feeling like a little kid, wanting to shout or hit something or someone. It's all ruined now. I really hate that.

I mean any change of plans. I actually hate any change. I guess you can call me sort of a nut, or maybe a conservative, but that's how I am.

To cheer myself up I begin to think of all the things we are going to do together, Kevin and I. For one thing we'll be playing lots of tennis. Dad got us a membership at the Forest Hills Club, which is about two blocks away, and that's one of the surprises we have for Kevin. The other big surprise is that we've got a box at Shea Stadium. It belongs to dad's boss, but whenever the Mets are playing during the day we can use it. Dad's boss can only make the night and weekend games. Another surprise is that mom is going to let us take her car up to Montreal to see Expo. I'll get to do some driving. That ought to be about the best part of summer.

Kevin probably didn't have much time for tennis so I can probably beat him, not that this matters to me. I'd actually rather lose to him. Even without practice Kevin is much better than I am, because he has a winning streak in him and I don't. It really surprised me when I got to the finals of the Queens Doubles this year. I got my picture in the paper, which isn't such a big deal, but it pleased mom. She showed it to all the ladies in her bridge club. The photographer didn't even get my name right, he spelled it Donaherr, but it didn't faze mom. The whole deal just embarrassed me.

Between tennis and baseball and Expo, I only hope we'll have enough time to go to Manhattan and Coney Island and maybe Fire Island. I really want this summer to be just one great ball for Kevin and me. Mom and dad understand that. They know that neither one of us intends to work this summer. Both Kevin and I have worked summers ever since we were fourteen, but this summer is going to be different. We'll be busy having fun.

But it's not doing things that will be the best part of it. It's just being with Kevin, talking with him and listening to him, that I'm looking forward to. It's been such a long time since I found out what he thinks about things like Viet Nam and the riots and President Johnson. I really want his opinions on these things so they can become my opinions, too.

If that sounds stupid or queer, I don't care. He's always right on things like that, and I don't want to get my point of view loused up by *Time* magazine or even by dad. I mean, dad is O.K. but he's middle-aged, for God's sakes, and to tell the truth he's not as smart as Kevin. So why shouldn't I be influenced by Kevin?

A couple of times he got mad at me about that. I guess I must have sort of quoted him directly without giving him credit, and he shouted at me: "Why don't you think for yourself? Why must you always repeat what I say?"

We almost had an argument, but I told him, without feeling ashamed or anything, that he's such a fabulously bright guy that I'd just as soon let him do my thinking as long as I was a kid.

It was all right after I told him that. He sort of messed up my hair and apologized for yelling at me. I know I sometimes embarrass him and I don't like to do that. But the way I figure it, he's my idol and he's got to pay the price. O.K., that's about all I'm going to write about that. I better go to sleep now anyway.

I've been rereading these last couple of pages, and I do sound sort of creepy. Worse than that, I'm making him sound like that.

You'd never believe it! My life is always being loused up by some stupid detail. What happened was the alarm clock didn't go off. I probably forgot to pull the damn button. Anyway, I was supposed to wake up mom and dad so we could go to pick up Kevin. At seven I finally woke up and rushed out of my bedroom. I found both mom and dad asleep in the living room with the television still going. I hardly looked at them. I just went straight over to Kevin's room. There was a hotel sign DO NOT DISTURB on his doorknob but that didn't stop me. I just barged in. There he was, asleep, with his mouth slightly open and his eyes not quite closed. When I was a little kid I used to be scared of that, of the way he could sleep with his eyes almost open. Anyway, I shook him by the shoulders, laughing like crazy, just being happy that he was there. When he did open his eyes wide enough to see me he groaned and covered his face. I pulled the sheet off him. He pulled it right back, half-shouting, half-groaning.

"Oh, God, leave me alone!"

"Do you mean it?" I asked.

"Yes, yes, I mean it! Later! Please let me sleep."

I got out of his room. I tried not to feel bad. After all he was probably dead tired waiting at that crummy airport and everything. On the way through the living room, I looked at mom and dad. They seemed sort of vulnerable, sleeping there, all dressed, with the light just barely hitting them through the closed drapes. I watched them for a while. They both looked older somehow and it depressed me. I'd never noticed how many wrinkles dad has around his eyes. And mom's chin sort of sagged, and her hair was thinning a little from all those permanents and the coloring jobs she gets. By the time I got to the kitchen to fix myself some breakfast I was so depressed I was almost crying, for God's sakes. I got to thinking that pretty soon they'll both get old and that one day they will both die.

I was halfway through scrambling some eggs when they came into the kitchen, looking sheepish instead of being mad at me for not waking them. That sort of undepressed me and we began to talk. I felt this funny thing in my stomach, being afraid for them growing old and dying and loving them at the same time. Anyway, I told them that Kevin was in his room and wanted to sleep. Mom wanted to know how he looked, whether he lost weight and junk like that.

It's about eleven now and he is still asleep and we're all waiting for him to get up. I'm in my room writing this, and I can see the backyard where mom is puttering around in her vegetable garden. She kneels down to get some weeds, then she seems to forget what she bent down for, and she gets to her feet and looks as if she was lost and then walks back into the house. Dad started out by cleaning some junk out of the basement, which I was supposed to do last Saturday, but he gives up too. I hear them talking to each other and walking around. Time just goes so slowly for all of us.

Lunch seemed late enough to be dinner. Kevin still wasn't up.

By four o'clock I couldn't wait any longer. I went into Kevin's room, without knocking or anything. I figured I'd just sit by his bed for a while and watch him sleep, but he wasn't asleep. He was sitting on the edge of his bed with his head in his hands, and I thought that he was either crying or sick and I got scared. I just stood there for a while with the horrible feeling that there was something terribly wrong with him. He hadn't even heard me come in.

"Hi, Kevin," I finally said.

He looked up and I was shocked. This morning I hadn't noticed that he looked different. But now I could see that he did. His eyes were very strange, wild and burning, and there was a sharpness to his face. He looked sort of old, and not at all well. All I could think of was how worried mom was going to be. He must have noticed I looked scared because he smiled, and then as if he could guess my thoughts, he said:

"I'll tell mom that I worked hard over the exams. Do I really look like hell?"

"Yeah, you do," I said. "What's wrong?"

He got off the bed and started to pace around, not saying anything, and his face was half hidden because he kept lifting up his skinny shoulders. After a while he stopped in front of me and tried to smile but he didn't do a very good job of it.

"What's wrong?" I asked again.

He started laughing. He wasn't laughing loudly or anything, but he was almost hysterical.

"What's wrong?" He repeated it about five times, laughing the whole time he said it. And then suddenly he stopped laughing and looked almost normal.

"How've you been, shrimp?" He used to call me that when I was just a kid.

"I've been O.K. I missed you."

"You did?"

"What the hell do you think?" I laughed. "You think a whole year goes by and I don't even miss you?"

"I've missed you too."

22

"How come you never came home for Thanksgiving or Christmas or spring vacation? How come? How come?"

"Cut it out, will you," Kevin says, and I know this bugs him, my getting carried away like a stupid kid. "Will you cut out repeating things? Why don't you wait for me to answer?"

"O.K., O.K.," I say, looking down at my shoes and feeling like a real jerk. I didn't like him talking to me like an adult. He used to criticize me a lot but he never used to sound like an adult. I decided to change the subject.

"Hey, how was the University of Chicago?" I asked him. "Did you have a real great time? How did you make out with the girls and everything?"

We hardly ever talk about girls. He feels that it's a private affair if you've got one and a creepy subject if you don't. Anyway I make up for not talking with him about sex by talking to the guys. Sometimes at the Wigwam that's about all we talk about.

"What do you think a university is like?" he asks me.

"I don't know," I say. "But you must have had a ball. Is that why you didn't come home?"

"No," he says, "that wasn't why."

He sat down on the bed. He looked at me for what seemed like a long time and I began to feel uneasy. I figure he wants to tell me something but doesn't know if he can trust me or not. Well if I can't be trusted, who the hell can? But I didn't pressure him or anything. I just waited for him to speak.

Then all of a sudden he smiled and said: "How old are you anyway?"

That was a silly question. He knows damn well so I didn't bother answering him.

"Sixteen," he said as if to himself. "Don't you ever grow up?"

"Come on," I said. "I can never catch up to you. I'll always be three stupid years behind you."

"At sixteen I knew next to nothing," he said. "Sixteen . . . what do you know at sixteen?"

"Plenty," I said. That was a silly lie about him not knowing anything at my age. He has always been a genius.

"Can I talk to you?" he asked. He really didn't know! My own brother Kevin was asking me that!

"Sure," I said. "You can talk to me. You can tell me anything, and you know I wouldn't tell mom and dad. You're not worrying about that, are you?"

He didn't say anything, and I began to get this wild idea. I imagined that he had gotten married. It must have been some movie I'd seen on TV or something, but honestly I could just see the girl huddled up, waiting at the airport. I thought, Oh hell, he's made her wait at the airport until he could tell the family.

Kevin still didn't answer me. But he was looking at me sort of funny.

"I'm your best friend," I said. "Don't you remember, you used to call me your best buddy? If you can't tell something to your best buddy, who can you tell it to?"

"Hey," Kevin said all of a sudden. "You ever been around anyone who smoked grass?"

"Grass?"

"Yeah, tea, pot, marijuana."

"You kidding," I said, and the girl waiting at the airport disappeared right out of my mind. "I've never taken any of that junk."

"I didn't ask you if you took it," Kevin says. "I asked you if you've been around anyone who did."

24

"I don't think so. Why?"

He sort of giggled then.

"One day you ought to get high," he said. "One day I'm going to make sure you get high."

"Hey, that would be tuff," I said but I didn't mean it. I'd been reading stuff about all that sort of junk—pot and LSD—and I'm scared of it. Just the other day I watched a TV program with addicts, and I couldn't even watch it to the end. People who use things like that depress the hell out of me.

He started laughing again and he sounded hysterical again. I mean he's never acted strange in his life before.

"You've been sold the scare propaganda," he says. "I can see they've really gotten to you. Boy, did they ever do a good job on you."

"Who?" I ask. "What are you talking about?"

"The Establishment," he says.

"Have you been on that junk?" I ask, feeling square.

"I really would like to turn you on," he says and smiles. "I really would like to see you wiped out."

"What do you mean wiped out?"

"High," he says, "on grass."

"O.K. Then give me some, if you've got it." I really didn't mean it at all. I wished he'd get off the subject. I wished he'd never started talking about that junk.

"I've got some stashed away," he says. "I couldn't make this scene without it. I'm all up tight about seeing the folks. I don't know what they're going to think."

"You're not going to tell them about the grass, are you?"

"No, of course not. But I want to stay high. I'd like to stay high all summer. How am I going to manage that? They're going to wise up to it."

"You're kidding," I said. This time I'm really angry at him. "Are you addicted to that stuff? Are you an addict?"

He laughed and looked around his room in a wild way.

"I don't know, man, I don't know where I'm at." He looks away from me and then he says, "I've taken trips but they got me nowhere."

"What do you mean trips? Do you mean LSD?"

"You dig. Acid."

"That stuff is dangerous, for God's sakes."

"Come off it," he says and tries to laugh but this time he doesn't quite make it. He suddenly gets real depressed and keeps mumbling to himself. I can't stand seeing him like that. What the hell did they do to him in Chicago?

About three months ago some guy came to our school. The guy was talking about the dangers of drugs, how marijuana can start you off on other junk. He said that people on heroin never get cured. He said it was a fact, but no one wants to admit it because then there would be no hope for the addicts. He showed us slides of how they end up in prisons or the morgue or in hospitals for life. By the end of the assembly period the whole student body except for some tough seniors looked as if they'd been scared right out of their minds. I know I was.

And now I realize that Kevin might be like one of those people the guy was talking about. He had already tried pot and LSD. He might go on to heroin, and then he'd be lost forever. I got real panic stricken. My shirt got soaking wet from sweat.

Before he left home he had this marvelous sort of humor about everything. I mean he used to kid a lot, and laugh a lot, and just have fun. Sometimes he could be mean, but funny-mean. That's because he called himself a cynic, which he really never was, I don't think.

But now, there he was, just sitting on the edge of his bed, looking as if he could never laugh about anything again. And I didn't know what I could do or say to him. But I guessed the last thing he wanted from me was help. And how the hell could I help him anyway when all I felt was this great fear for him? It took all the control I had not to run out of the room and tell mom and dad.

He lay down on his bed and closed his eyes and I thought he was going to go to sleep again, but he started to talk. He talked in a sort of drone and I had to strain to hear.

"When I got to Chicago I was up tight about everything. I couldn't figure it out really, because I did want to get away from home and be on my own. But maybe that's what made me scared, being on my own. Anyway I was walking around scared all the time until I got in with a bunch of kids who were playing it very cool. They'd sit around talking, mostly against everything, especially studying. We'd go to the movies instead of classes and pretty soon we began to smoke pot. Every day."

I wanted to interrupt him but he went on. The way he talked it was as if he was reciting something, not really telling me what happened to him, that was the strangest thing about it. It was so impersonal, as if it didn't concern him.

"Before Christmas I got tired of them. I wanted to be alone when I smoked grass. So I rented a room by myself and just stayed there. At first it was really great being alone. I was high on grass most of the time, but I still felt up tight. And that was bad. Feeling that way all the time and having dreams. I mean I slept a lot, and I'd always have those nightmares . . ."

"What kind of nightmares?" I asked. But he didn't answer me.

"I got more and more depressed. And all the time I was thinking of taking acid. But I didn't do it. I didn't do it until spring. It wasn't that I was scared of it, it's just that by then I really was living all alone, like a hermit. I just didn't see anyone who'd sell me acid. I didn't see anyone at all. I just stayed in my room."

"You mean you didn't even go to classes?" I asked.

He looked at me as if he was surprised that I was there. And he sat up in bed and smiled at me.

"You don't have to if you don't want to," he said.

"You're kidding!"

"You have to keep up, though. And you take tests. But as long as you pass them you don't have to make the classroom scene. Anyway, I just got so damn used to being in my room. It was like . . . well, a sort of a warm, safe place where nobody bugged me."

He leaned his head against the wall and stopped talking for a while and I was looking at him, imagining him in that room. It was the saddest thing I've ever imagined, him alone in that room.

"What happened?" I asked. "What happened when you took that stuff?"

"What happened?" He laughed and shrugged his shoulders. "I don't really know what happened. I was at an acid party. There were a bunch of people who were digging what was happening to them, and all I felt was tuned out. All I saw was emptiness inside and emptiness on the outside. It was the most horrible feeling. You're supposed to 'turn on, tune in, and drop out.' I didn't tune in. Maybe the kids I was with did it.

But not me. . . ." He got off the bed and walked to the window and looked out.

He stood with his back to me and I wanted very badly to know what made him want to take that stuff the second time. But I waited for him to tell me and he did. He turned around and he looked real sad.

"The second time I was alone and . . . I wanted to kill myself."

"Oh, no!"

"I don't know why I didn't do it. I really wanted to. You know what drove me crazy enough to want to do it?" He came back and sat on his bed again. "I kept feeling that there was a door I was supposed to go through. The thing was I didn't know where it was or how I could find it or if I would have enough guts to go through it. It was awful, not knowing. But next time . . ."

"Next time?" I shouted at him. "You can't do it again!"

"Who says I can't? I'll do it again. And I'll find the door and go through it. And there won't be any circles to stop me either."

"What circles?"

He got off the bed and started to unpack his suitcase.

"What circles?"

"I'll tell you some other time," he said. "I've got to shave before I see mom and dad."

I followed him into the bathroom. I wanted to tell him all sorts of things and ask him all kinds of questions. Most of all I wanted to shout at him for being stupid and ruining his life with those drugs. But he wouldn't have listened. So I waited for a while to cool off and then I said:

"You're home now. It's different from being away. You won't need any of that stuff. Besides, in school you're

29

bound to have problems. But here, where you belong, this summer, you're not going to have any. Except keeping me out of your hair. But listen, dad got us into the tennis club. We can play every day, if you want to. And we have a free box at Shea Stadium for the day games. And mom is letting us use her car to go to Expo."

It was sort of cruddy of me to tell him all that. We were all going to do it together, mom and dad and me.

Those were the surprises we had saved for him.

There was a knock on the door and mom and dad piled into the bathroom and the hugging began. Kevin was doing all right. He was slapping dad on the back and lifting mom off her feet and they didn't notice anything was wrong with him.

"You look a little peaked," mom said. "You need rest and home cooking."

"He looks fine," dad said. "Don't fuss too much over him or he'll get a pot belly like me."

I couldn't stand it, so I rushed off to my room and started writing down everything Kevin said so far. I figure if I keep a really accurate record of everything it will help in finding a way for Kevin to be like he used to be before he went to Chicago. I have to help him do that. And I have to help him hide what has happened to him from mom and dad. Most of all I have to see to it that he doesn't take LSD again.

When I finished writing everything down I went to find Kevin. He was out on the front lawn with mom and dad, admiring the flower garden. Ever since we moved to Forest Hills both of them think we've got a farm, for God's sakes, the way they work out in that little bit of ground around our house. I noticed Kevin was wearing dark glasses and I was glad that they could not see the change in his eyes. Kevin was holding his hands in back of him. His right fingers were digging into the back of his left hand. I could tell he was under a horrible strain just *being* with mom and dad.

"How about a beer, son?" dad asked in this broadminded voice he sometimes uses. "I know how you college men drink. Or would you rather have something stronger?"

Kevin managed to laugh.

"I'll split a beer with you," he said. And his voice sort of shook. I think he was tempted to tell my dear, square father that it wasn't booze that the college men indulged in nowadays.

The amazing thing was that neither mom or dad were noticing anything. We all go inside to watch the ball game on TV and mom brings out a dip and potato chips and Kevin's beer and a Coke for me. We all sit down in front of the television set, and it's like old times. Except for Kevin. He must be going through hell. That's what I keep on thinking and it kills me. I know he isn't really in that room at all. And they see nothing wrong! It just breaks my heart.

Around the seventh inning I get real depressed. We used to be such a normal family. What the hell is happening to us? Kevin almost a junkie, me going practically out of my mind worrying about it, and mom and dad not seeing anything at all. Why did it have to happen to him? He was always so brilliant! He'd be the last person I know who'd need something phony like pot or LSD. He always had anything he wanted. He could be anything! God, in high school he barely needed to open a book to graduate with honors!

Anyway we've made it all right through the first day. We had dinner and then we all went to a movie together. Kevin said good-night first and I hung around to find out what mom and dad would say about him. All dad said was: "Isn't it grand to have him home?" And mom just worried some more about his lack of sleep and proper diet. But neither one seemed concerned about the terrible change in him.

God, I wish I could wake up tomorrow and Kevin would tell me that he was pulling my leg, and none of the things he said were true.

SUNDAY, JUNE 11

We were supposed to go see granddad today. He is living in this home. It's not really like an old people's place; it's more like a club. Anyway it's not really depressing. It's on Long Island and we visit him once a month, on a sort of regular basis.

It's fun for granddad where he is because he gets to do the things he likes most to do which is play cards and billiards. He even has a bar out there and an indoor swimming pool and everything. A couple of his old friends live there too. He has a bum heart and that's why he has to be around a doctor and nurses. He had I don't know how many coronaries. He once told me: "People's hearts are like watches. Some have expensive ones. Mine is a Mickey Mouse."

I love granddad. Not only because he is old. I admire him because he is tough. I mean strong, the way a man ought to be. Dad isn't like that and I sometimes wonder why since he's granddad's son. But I think Kevin is.

Anyway we were almost getting into the car when Kevin says:

"I better not go with you."

Mom right away looks panicky. She hates to have things change. I guess I get it from her. I mean we both hate the unexpected.

"What's wrong?" she asks Kevin and my heart is pounding because she is asking that question.

"It must have been something I ate," he says. "I've got to rush to the bathroom every few minutes. I better make it next time. Give my love to gramps."

"Well, we'll stay, too," mom says.

"Oh, no!" Kevin almost shouts. "You go on."

"I'll stay," I say suddenly. "You two go on. I'll stay with Kevin."

I really would much rather have gone with them. But I stayed.

The car was barely out of the driveway when Kevin begins to laugh and then puts his arm around my shoulder and says:

"O.K., shrimp, let's get high."

"What do you mean let's get high?"

"On grass, kid."

"I hate that stuff," I say. "I wish you'd lay off it."

"How can you hate something you don't know?"

What I really hate at that moment is the way he looks and sounds. Excited. Sort of dopey-eager. Like a wino who sees a handout coming. But all of a sudden I think that if I'm going to help him I'll have to learn what it is that I am saving him from. So I say to him:

"O.K., let's go."

My knees are shaking as we go into the house and my

throat is dry and I want to change my mind. If he were younger than me I could beat him up or threaten him, but what can I do to make him stop? Nothing.

In Kevin's bedroom all I can do is watch him. First he takes a little bag out of his suitcase and some cigarette paper, and then he starts looking for something among his shirts and stuff.

"Hey, you wouldn't have any incense, would you?" he asks me.

"Incense?"

"Yeah, it kills the smell of pot." He realizes I wouldn't have anything like that around and starts to giggle. "It's O.K.," he says. "I'll put on the fan after a while." I watch him as he rolls three cigarettes. They are much thinner than the regular kind. Although I'm very scared I begin to feel sort of excited.

"What do I do?" I ask.

"Try to sort of eat the smoke," he says.

"Eat it?"

"Yeah, don't exhale it. Once you inhale it, try to keep it down."

"I don't think I'll be able to do it." I hardly ever even smoke the regular cigarettes, for God's sakes. "I'll show you," he says.

"What is it going to do to me?" I ask him.

He laughs, but in his old way. And he looks so much better now, like his old self. And he sounds like he used to. And for a second I am very happy, but then I remember that it's because he is going to smoke pot. Just the idea of it makes him like that. And I feel furious, at him, at myself, and at the junk we are going to take. We shouldn't be doing it! We could get busted for doing it, for Christ's sakes.

"A pot smoker is a pleasure seeker," Kevin is saying.

34

"Remember that and stop worrying. Pleasure is all you can get from pot."

"Do you? Do you get pleasure from it?"

"Sure," he says.

"But you're not happy."

"I didn't say you get happiness from pot. I said pleasure."

He lights a cigarette and inhales it deeply and all I can see is a very thin, almost invisible, puff of smoke that escapes him. He hands the cigarette to me without saying a word and I inhale it, scared again. I'm scared of what it will do to me and scared by its sickly sweet smell. I try to keep all of the smoke down, and I give him back the cigarette because his hand is out for it. We don't speak at all as we smoke, passing the cigarette back and forth until the butt is so small that it burns my fingers. But he smokes it to the very end, holding it by his nails. And when that one is finished he lights another, and we start on that.

"How many are we going to smoke?" I ask. My head is beginning to feel funny.

"They're trying to make a religion out of it," he says, without answering my question. "And do you know something? When someone asked Voltaire how one can found a new religion, he said, 'Get yourself crucified and then rise on the third day.'"

He starts to giggle and he asks me whether I don't think that's funny. But I can't answer him, because all of a sudden something fantastic is happening to me. *I can see my mind!* I really, actually, can see the *structure* of my mind. It is a network of—I thought of the right words immediately—"celestial wires." It's magnificent! A thousand little threads, each with a reason for being there. They are so delicate and beautiful, I can't get over it. I say to myself, This is God's most perfect creation.

And I say to Kevin: "Is that what you see? Is that what you see?"

And he says: "What do you see?"

"My mind, my mind!" I want to describe it to him but I feel that I don't need to. I am sure that he sees what I see, and I feel good about that. "Is it always like that?" I ask. "Does everyone see the same thing?"

"Some people do, some don't," he says and his voice is coming to me before he speaks, as if my mind didn't have to hear to understand. And it's like another miracle.

"Will I feel everything that you feel?" I am not sure if I asked the question aloud. I don't think so. There wasn't any more need to speak. It was a very strange and a very wonderful thing.

"I doubt it." He didn't actually say this, but I heard him anyway. The possibilities of this talking without words knocks me out. This must be the "high" that he had talked about. It was incredible. We began to wordlessly "talk" to each other and everything we "say" now is terribly funny. Hilarious, actually. I can't remember now what was so funny, but I was laughing at everything. I was having the most wonderful time of my life because I've never been brilliant before and I was then. And my brilliance was coming so easily from that incredible, perfect mind of mine. I knew even then that it couldn't last, but I didn't care. I mean I wasn't feeling greedy about it or anything. It was all a very pure sort of thing. Unpolluted.

But suddenly the fun stopped. I felt the *presence* of someone else in the room. But there was no one else. Yet there was. It took me some time to be sure. But then I was sure of it. The presence was there, and it was evil.

I looked at Kevin. He was half-lying, half-sitting in a chair. His eyes were closed, and I thought that he felt the presence too. It was an effort to speak now but I spoke loudly, making my words very distinct. It was ages before I heard my own voice:

"Do you see him?"

"Who?"

"Someone. Someone evil."

"Don't be silly," he said, getting up and putting a Jefferson Airplane record on the phonograph.

"He is after you!" I shouted, jumping up and going to him. "You know that, Kevin. You must know that!"

It was so fantastically plain to me, the danger to him, but he just shook my hands off his shoulders. The music was blaring at top volume now and the fan kept going round and round and I tried to stop thinking but I couldn't! Suddenly I felt terribly dizzy and had to rush off to the bathroom.

I've never thrown up as bad as that before. The worst thing about it was hearing the retching. It was so loud that I couldn't hear anything else. It seemed that the sound had always been in my head, and that it would never stop for as long as I lived. But when I quit throwing up it did stop.

I staggered back to Kevin's room.

"You sure know how to cop out on pleasure," he said. I felt that he didn't want me in his room anymore and besides I was too ashamed of the sounds he must have heard to stay there.

It's really impossible to describe or to explain what happened next. I mean in real life you've got things like logic and common sense to fall back on. But with pot everything is off keel. Anyway, when I got to my room and closed the door, I thought I saw something else. *Another presence.* And the new presence was good.

There was a huge difference between the evil presence and the good presence. The evil presence was a real pro. But the good presence was like an amateur, without class. I remember thinking that they were unfair to send their number one man against a beginner. I didn't know who "they" were supposed to be, but that's what I thought.

"They've sent the best so it must matter a lot."

That thought, or those words, came from the good presence and I felt that I had to explain things so I said: "Sure it matters. We're going to fight for my brother." And then, just as I said it, I realized that I actually was about to fight for Kevin. Me and the good presence against the evil one. So I added, "We'll do the best we can. That's about all we can do."

It started then, a sort of deluge of thoughts. Evil thoughts and good thoughts, both. The evil thoughts were attacking Kevin and the good thoughts were defending him. The horrible thing was that sometimes I felt that I was responsible for both the evil and the good thoughts. It was just a suspicion but it almost drove me out of my mind. And it scared me because sometimes my "good" arguments weren't good enough and we were arguing about Kevin's worth as a human being.

"There is nothing special about him," the evil one seemed to say. *"And there never was."*

That got me real mad and I shouted that Kevin was the most worthwhile person I knew.

"How many people do you really know?"

"Many!"

"What makes him so special?"

I couldn't answer.

"What makes him so great?"

I couldn't answer that either. But suddenly the good presence prompted me.

"His soul! It's his soul that's so special. That's why we're fighting over it."

The minute he said this I understood what it was all about. The evil was not inside me and neither was the good. The good presence was actually an angel and the evil one was the devil. I don't know why I didn't see that right away. They were as real as people! I laughed because I was so relieved I didn't have to be scared anymore about going crazy. I even joked with the angel then.

"How do you rank in heaven?" I asked him.

"From the bottom?"

I laughed and I think he did too.

"About tenth," he said. He seemed embarrassed and added: "See, there are younger guys . . ."

But I was so exhausted then that he stopped talking.

I stretched out on my bed. As soon as my head touched the pillow I felt myself falling into a pit. I was falling down and down into an inverted cone. Everything inside of the cone was red.

The next thing I knew I was standing in front of a big curving desk with a lot of men in red robes sitting behind it. I could not see their faces and I don't know how come, but I knew that this was the high command of hell, the big shots, their generals and senators and judges. I got very scared because they were old and wise and they knew all there was to know. How could I possibly win against them?

"Don't let them bother you," my angel whispered. He was not around, yet I heard that thought coming from

him and I was really grateful for it. The men in red were talking about Kevin. I either couldn't understand what they said or wasn't really listening. But suddenly I realized that they were acting as if Kevin was theirs, as if he belonged to them. And I screamed at them that they don't have him, that they never will.

I had rushed closer to them and was pounding my fist against that big desk that separated them from me. My fists were coming down and making dents in it and I knew it was made of cardboard. And then I looked more closely at their robes and noticed they were nothing but paper. And I began to laugh.

The idea that hell could be that cheap and shoddy just broke me up. And the more I laughed the smaller the devils became, and then they disappeared altogether. It was marvelous, right after that, after I made hell disappear. My angel was back with me and we were both laughing like crazy.

"Hell's just a barbeque pit," I laughed. "And all those big shots are nothing but a bunch of phonies dressed in Halloween costume rejects."

The thing was, it wasn't a dream or anything. All of this was really *happening*.

I thought it was all over then. But suddenly the devil was back again, mocking Kevin, calling him an addict and "a lost soul." And it seemed that my victory in hell had not happened at all. And there was something new now. A sense of great danger. I could hear brakes screeching. I didn't know whether the sound came from the street or from inside my mind. But I knew that wherever mom and dad were at this moment they were in danger of an accident.

"No!" I shouted. "You leave them alone! You can't touch them!"

40

"*Why not?*" the devil asked. "*We have the power to destroy them.*"

"You cantyoucantyoucant!" I shouted over and over again as the screech continued. "Leave my parents alone!"

It seemed like a long time before the screech of the brakes died down and before the devil spoke.

"*What do you have?*" he asked finally. "*What do you have that would be worth your parents' lives?*"

Maybe it was my angel or maybe it was me, but the answer came at the same time that the question was asked.

"I can give you my mind."

I thought the devil would laugh, but he didn't. I guess that my offer was accepted because the feeling of danger disappeared. And again I felt that I had won a round.

I felt terribly tired. All this time I was lying down on my bed, but it seemed as if I had been physically struggling. All I wanted was to sleep, to rest. And I was nearly asleep when the devil spoke again.

"*Kevin's mind already belongs to us.*"

I let out a whole bunch of swear words then, words I didn't think I knew, and then I shouted:

"Take my soul and leave Kevin alone!"

The moment I said this I knew that Kevin was saved. I was dead sure of it. All this time this is what had been expected of me, to trade my own soul for his. But I was not frightened of what I had done. I felt real peaceful and closed my eyes.

The next thing I knew I was hearing mom's voice: "Jimmy, dinner's ready!" And then the sound of the doorknob and, "Why did you lock yourself in?"

I couldn't face them. I had a headache and I felt sick to my stomach again.

"I don't feel like eating," I said, hoping that my voice sounded all right. It seemed to be coming back at me from the other side of the room.

"Maybe you got sick on the same thing Kevin ate," mom said. "How about some broth? Or Bromo?"

"No thanks, mom."

"Won't you let me in?"

"I'm in bed." I looked at my watch and it was only eight o'clock.

"All right, dear, but if you get hungry or want anything . . ."

"I'll let you know. And thanks, mom."

She didn't notice anything wrong. I guess parents never notice anything important.

I lay in bed, not asleep, and not even trying to think anymore, just waiting for the high to go away. I hated that feeling, all rubbery and dizzy, with my thoughts still crisscrossing as if they were a whole bunch of Ping-Pong balls all around me. I couldn't *see* my mind anymore, or the devil, or the angel. What happened to my angel, I wondered. I never had a chance to thank him.

"You were on trial and you did all right."

He had not gone away. My angel was still around.

"It wasn't me. It was Kevin who was on trial," I reminded him.

"No, it was you," my angel insisted. *"Your soul was on trial."*

"But I gave it away," I said.

"You made the offer to give it away."

And that was that. He left for good and I was alone to figure things out by myself. I got out of bed and started writing all this down. The way I see it is that what happened was something like a judgement. "He will come to judge the living and the dead . . ." I've been judged. And I guess I must have passed the judgement. But that was not what I wanted to do. What I meant to do was to save Kevin.

MONDAY, JUNE 12

I think I was still high as I slept last night. I had at least a couple dozen dreams going at the same time, a real madhouse. I woke up with a headache but after I took a shower it went away enough for me to read over everything I wrote down last night. I couldn't make out all the words. My handwriting looks pretty shaky.

What I had written down doesn't sound quite right. First of all how could I possibly describe something that I thought I saw but actually didn't see at all, like the angel and the devil? And all the other sensations? How could I describe them? But more than that I didn't even bother describing the horror of it. It was horrible, all that evil, and not knowing if I could stand up against its power. And there was horror in not being able to control thoughts and what would happen next. And there was horror in all the unknown things that I was experiencing. I didn't get all that down. And the other thing that was missing was when I was so brilliant, at the beginning. I mean I really was very funny but I can't remember that part at all. Maybe I wasn't all that smart, maybe it was a sort of an illusion.

Anyway that was the strangest and the most unforgettable experience I've ever had. But I wouldn't want to go through anything like that again. And it's not that I'd be scared, though I would be, but I wouldn't want to get high again for one reason. I'm myself and I am stuck with that. I don't like being someone I don't know; I don't want to be uprooted from how I have to live. And pot did all that to me.

When I came down to breakfast it was after ten and I figured Kevin would still be asleep. Mom left a note on the icebox:

GONE SHOPPING AND THEN TO BRIDGE LUNCHEON. BE BACK AROUND FOUR. HAM IN THE ICEBOX. IF YOU GO SOMEWHERE I'LL EXPECT YOU BACK FOR DINNER UNLESS YOU CALL. LOVE, MOTHER.

I was still reading it when Kevin came in. He was still in his pajamas and he looked pretty awful. His eyes were so dead and his face had that old-man look to it. I began to apologize to him, feeling stupid, about how badly I took to pot.

"I'm just a square, I guess," I said. I wanted to tell him all about what had happened when I was high and I wanted to ask him what it was like for him. But he didn't want to talk about it.

"You're O.K.," he said. "You're one of those people who get high on life and things and don't need other stuff."

"But you used to get high on life too."

"Yeah, I used to," he said and sat down at the kitchen table. "Got some coffee ready?"

He certainly wasn't in the best of moods. All I could

do was try to cheer him up. I told him a couple of stories I've recently heard, which I thought were pretty funny in a stupid way, but he didn't even crack a smile. He just sat there drinking his coffee, looking real defeated. I had not helped him at all, I thought desperately. His life was so loused up how could he possibly care about his soul?

This soul, angel, and devil business is sort of strange. I used to be a very religious kid just before and after I made my First Communion. We're Catholics, not really fanatical or anything, and dad usually complains about the Church and our parish priests, but when I was about seven and eight I used to really dig God and His saints. It really gave me a big charge to be learning about Jesus. I thought He was the neatest person who had ever lived. I sort of went nutty at one point and talked to Him and to the saints in church. But lately I've just been going to Mass more out of habit than anything and I've been worrying how little it all means to me. Kevin had always been very fair and even in his feelings about religion. He once said to me that he needed religion more than his religion needed him. "The Church," he said, "gives me the logical answers to questions I am interested in. So I can't knock it." But we really never discussed God, as we've never really discussed girls.

As we sat in the kitchen I wanted to ask Kevin if it was at all possible, if it made any sense at all, that one could go through a judgement while under the influence of pot. Ever since I got up this morning, and was rereading my notebook, I've been thinking about that. I mean out of everything that I remember happening yesterday I am most proud of what my angel told me. I really believe I did save my soul, for the moment, anyway. And I wanted Kevin to tell me it was so.

But just as I was about ready to phrase the question, he spoke up:

"Know anyone around here who sells acid?"

That really got me mad.

"Come on, come off it, Kevin!" I yelled at him.

"Don't yell at me," he said quietly, his eyes steely. "I shouldn't have asked you anyway," he said pushing his chair away. "I should have known you wouldn't understand."

I reached him before he reached the kitchen door.

"But I do," I said very earnestly, "I do understand and I'd do anything—" I was going to say to help him but he interrupted me.

"Forget it, kid."

I followed him into the living room. He sank into a chair and closed his eyes. I had to find out about him! I had to know what made him change. I just couldn't bear to see him so dejected.

"Please don't shut me out," I begged.

He didn't say anything for a while, and when he spoke I barely could hear him, his voice was so low.

"It's all circles, it's all made of circles. Hey, do you know how to get out of a circle?" He didn't wait for my answer. I didn't have an answer, of course. I didn't even know what he meant. "It's a losing game. With a maze you've got at least a chance, but how do you escape from a circle? That bad trip I went on, that was the most truth I've ever seen."

He got up and began to pace in front of me, and his voice rose when he continued.

"See, shrimp, it's this way for me. I've got those circles around me. They start at my feet and they go up to my shoulders. If they ever reach my neck—and they will. They will!—I'll choke."

He was at the window pushing aside the drapes and looking out on our street.

"We're nowhere," he said suddenly and angrily. "That dumb street, this house! This whole," and he swore then and I've never heard him use that word before, "country, the whole damn scene!"

He sprawls over the sofa and doesn't let me ask him what he had meant about the circles. He is on a talk marathon or something. He used to get like that, except that before he was always so crystal clear, and now some of his words are mumbled and most of his thoughts seem so confused.

"I've gotten tired, man, from understanding what I didn't want to understand. What's the use? What was ever the use? Man, do I ever want out! I don't want to have any connection with this world. None. Not a one. Like pfffft . . . me and the world, we're splitsville. But how the hell does one kick the habit of living? It's tough. I can isolate myself pretty well. I've become a sort of a master at it, you might say. Alienated, they call it. You just stand with your eyes away from the street and the parade goes by, on its own."

"Do you mean to say," I interrupted, "that you want to cop out on everything?"

"You're so right, man, you're so right! I don't want to take either the credit or the blame. I'm not even asking for a refund on my life. All I want is to be left out."

"What do you mean? You mean out of everything, your country and your family . . ."

"The world, the mess, the everything. They did it all wrong."

"Who is they?"

"The Establishment, the stinking Establishment . . .

hey, do you know who killed President Kennedy?"
"Oswald."
"Wrong! The Establishment. Man, were they slow in catching up to him! He opened doors while they were asleep. But when they smelled the fresh air that he let in they killed him. Those old men want everything to die. . . ."
"One stupid, jackass punk killed Kennedy," I said.
"Man, you're nowhere." He turned on the television set and that made me real mad. I went over and turned it off and then I sort of began to yell at him:
"You've got to live in this world. It's the only one we've got. And if you don't like it as it is, change it! You could do it, you could do anything. President Kennedy was your hero and you can't act as if he never lived. Besides, he wanted everybody to get involved! Remember what he said about 'It isn't what your country . . .'"
"He is dead."
"So what if he's dead? Most of the great guys are dead, Bogart is, and Cooper, Lincoln and Jefferson . . ."
He was laughing now and this time he was laughing at me. Maybe it was sort of stupid of me to dump movie stars with presidents and things, but that's not what he minded.
"Man, did they ever brainwash you," he said.
"Nobody brainwashed me!"
"Mister Clean couldn't have done a better job! You're such a square, clean-cut kid you still think everything's fine and dandy with the world. You haven't even noticed that everything's changed. You don't even smell the rottenness that's all around you."
"There is nothing rotten around me except what they've done to you."
"Who?"

"How the hell should I know? Maybe the junkies you were palling around with. They turned you into a crazy . . ." I couldn't think of the word. I wanted to tell him that he had a persecution complex or something.

"You and Mary Poppins, you're both for mental health."

I had about enough from him by then.

"You know something," I said, "I better start thinking for myself. You've got nothing to teach me anymore." That must have hurt him and I was sorry I said it the moment I did. If he wasn't sick then he was in trouble and I had no right to hurt his feelings.

"I'm sorry," I said. "I didn't mean that." He didn't say anything. "Hey, do you want to toss a ball around in the driveway?" I asked him. He used to love pitching to me.

"No," he said.

"What do you want to do then?"

"I think I'll go over to the Village," he said, getting off the sofa. "I'm going to get dressed."

"O.K. I'll come with you."

I am sure he didn't plan to take me along. But I intend to stick pretty close to him.

On the way over to the subway I asked him if he had changed his mind about his major in college which was going to be political science.

"You see me as President of the United States?" he asked.

"Sure, why not?"

"Politicians grow richer as the world gets more rotten."

"Come on, how about your Kennedy?"

"Kennedy was different. He didn't need to get rich and he had us going not for but against the world. It will never happen again."

"It will too!" I didn't quite know what he was talking about but I wasn't going to let him wipe out my future.

"There are a couple more Kennedys . . ."

"I don't know about them. I can't smell them out and I don't think I want to bother."

"I think they're good guys. I don't think you can come from the same family and have one good brother and one rotten . . ."

He slapped me on the shoulder and laughed again. "Sure you can," he said. "Look at us."

"I'm not rotten!"

"But I am."

"You're not! You're just confused." I didn't mean to patronize him. He looked away and I knew he wouldn't be listening anymore. But that didn't stop me. "You're saying dumb things now because you take this idiot stuff that scrambles your brain. And I think it's too bad that you, of all people, think you have to take something like that."

I wasn't good enough, I realized. I wasn't bright or clever enough to interest him, to make him listen to me, and he was nice enough not to make fun of my attempts to straighten him out. The awful thing was, I sounded like dad and I didn't mean to. As we walked into the subway he messed up my hair and said: "You're the good guy and I'm the bad guy. Let's leave it at that." And then he did something that I always used to love. He imitated James Cagney. And not any old line but my very most favorite: "How you doing, Parker. . . . You want some air? . . . I'll give you some air."

That's from the movie "White Heat" where Cagney plays Cody Jarrett and it's one of the old-time greats.

When he says that line he's speaking to this guy who tried to rub him out in prison and who's now in the trunk of this car and he's eating, Cody I mean, this chicken leg. And then he puts about four plugs into the trunk and walks away still eating the chicken leg. Boy, was that ever a great movie!

And then, Kevin says the other great line that Cody has:

"And I was going fifty-fifty with a copper!"

It really sends me, hearing Kevin do Cagney. He is so great at it, hunching his shoulders and moving the way he does, and his voice is exactly right and he remembers almost all of Cagney's lines, I mean, from every picture we've ever seen.

One of the best things we used to do together was watching old movies on television. We were so hooked on them that whenever they'd have a real great one on during the day we'd pretend to be sick and we'd stay home from school just to see it.

And there was something else we used to do which we did now. Whenever we used to ride the subway together, we'd go up front to the first car. We'd stand looking out of the front window into the blackness ahead and the lit-up stations. The express trains are the greatest, because you get to go past the local stops. The people standing on those local platforms always look real neat, sort of suspended in time, like they lived in some Twilight Zone or something.

And that's what we did now. We got into the front car. There were a couple of little kids standing at the front window so we sort of leaned over them hoping they'd go away. And they did. I guess they didn't like us breathing down their necks. When I was small and a bigger kid would do that I wouldn't budge, but I was always scared of getting hit or even knifed or something. I think there were more hoods in those days than there are now. Or maybe now the hoods are sitting around someplace, smoking pot or taking LSD and are off the streets and out of subways.

"Hey, this is fun," Kevin said when the kids moved away and we had the window to ourselves.

"Sure it's fun," I said, and then, I say one of my favorite lines: "This seems to me like a lot of supernatural baloney."

And Kevin comes right back and, in this great Hungarian accent that Bela Lugosi has, he says: "Supernatural, perhaps. Baloney, perhaps not."

And we both laugh like crazy. Those lines are from my favorite horror movie "The Black Cat." The movie wasn't that great or anything but it was the first one that Boris Karloff made together with Bela Lugosi. And that makes it pretty much of a classic as far as I'm concerned.

When we still lived in Manhattan, just before moving to Forest Hills, we used to be real crazy about westerns, especially the ones with John Wayne. We'd pretend our bikes were horses, and we'd jump off them as if we were going to tie them up to hitching posts. And mom was always the schoolmarm in those days and dad was the banker, our house was the saloon, the school was a jail, and our room was an abandoned gold mine or a hideout. Later, when we moved, we went through the gangster craze and I developed a real great sneer. Kevin's upper lip was never as flexible as mine, and I used to be real proud of mine, and would stand in front of the mirror for hours just sneering. Boy, was I ever a jackass in those days. But funny as it might seem, I really miss those days when we'd be living in the twenties and thirties, and acting silly all the time. And as we were riding in the subway that's what I wanted to do again.

"Hey," I said, "who should we pretend to be?"

"What do you mean?" Kevin asked.

He must have been lost in his own dark thoughts by then. He must have completely forgotten that just a while back he did a great Cagney as Cody Jarrett and then the Bela Lugosi bit. I didn't answer him because I was so pissed off at him forgetting. He looked at me and smiled and then said: "Do you want me to do a Herbert Marshall?"

He did the greatest Herbert Marshall, but always for laughs, not really seriously or as a game. And that was his solo performance. I couldn't play anyone then, when he was doing Marshall.

"I want to play too," I said.

"Why don't you do your John Garfield while I do my Marshall?" he said.

That was my solo bit with the curling lip. I did Garfield pretty well if I do say so myself.

"No," I said, "let's do something together. I'll be Peter Lorre and you do Bogey. O.K.?"

We used to do that a lot together. That was about my favorite combination.

"All right," he said, but I knew he didn't really want to play. Besides, we were at 59th Street by then, and the shoppers from Bloomingdale's and Alexander's were piling into the train. From here on, the subway wasn't much fun. And suddenly I got very depressed. Sometimes I get so depressed that I get to worrying about my mental health, for God's sakes. I mean I seem to sort of die of depression and it's a pretty scary feeling. Anyway the reason I got so depressed then was that suddenly I thought that the reason Kevin wanted to come to the Village was to pick up some LSD. As I looked up at him he must have seen how depressed I was because he smiled at me and messed up my hair and said:

"You look like a lost Mouseketeer."

"What's that?" I said.

"Don't you remember those creepy kids on television who used to sit around with mouse hats on?"

"Yeah," I said and laughed. I sort of vaguely remembered a real dumb TV show.

"You must have been around four or something," Kevin was saying. "How come you remember that far back?"

"Don't you remember things that far back?" I asked him.

His face clouded over. And all of a sudden I remembered something. Just before he left for Chicago he was going to tell me something that happened when he was five and I was only two. He never did tell me. So I asked him now.

"Forget it, kid," he said. He calls me kid only when he wants me to drop the subject. So I did. But it didn't stop me from wondering, though. What could it have been?

A few months ago dad brought a doctor home for dinner, a psychoanalyst. He had this thick German accent and I wasn't listening too hard to what he said. But at one point this guy said something that really interested me. He said that what shapes our characters and personalities, and what also makes for most of our problems later on in life, are things that happen to us when we are little children.

That got me to thinking. What if when he was five Kevin tried to kill me for instance? I mean it's sort of farfetched, but a lot of kids resent babies coming into

54

the family. Maybe Kevin just hated me for a little while and sort of wished I was dead. And maybe, over the years, he felt so guilty about it that he felt he had to make it up to me by being so great to me? Anyway I was going to write him about this and I was going to tell him that I don't mind it, him hating me when he was just a kid, but I never got around to writing him about that.

Anyway that's what I was thinking about now, trying to decide whether to talk to him about it and make him mad or to forget about it all. But what if that was one of the things that got him in the shape he was in? I don't know, maybe I am just a coward but I couldn't bring myself to say anything about it. If he liked me all along I'd only make a fool of myself, and if he did hate me once he probably doesn't even remember it now.

He looked sort of angry anyway. Angry and alone. What did he say he was, alienated? Hell, I read somewhere about that, how college kids get that way. I wish I could remember what the article said about it and whether there was a cure for it or something. The trouble with me is that I read about a million things, the magazines mom and dad subscribe to, books from the library and the book clubs, ads on the subway, even junk you find in dentists' offices and at the barber shop. But I hardly ever remember what I've read. I'm really a slob. Intellectually speaking, that is.

We hardly said a word between the 59th Street stop and Sheridan Square, and by the time we got out of the subway I was feeling really guilty and ashamed. What was I doing here anyway? I was actually spying on Kevin and being a sort of a guardian to him. Maybe all he wanted to do was see the old stinking Village again, maybe he didn't even think of LSD and stuff like that. I tried to act real casual, sort of swaggering around and looking into store windows. A couple of times I stuck out my foot to trip someone but it didn't work. As we passed Fourth Street I asked Kevin where we were going.

"MacDougal, I guess," he said and hurried on. I hadn't been to the Village in a few months and the place had really changed. It looked like some kind of a psychedelic Coney Island, for God's sakes. In the afternoon, with not too many people around, except for some middle-aged looking people taking a walk, it was all so shoddy and cheap. Years ago, when Kevin and I used to ride our bikes around this place the tourists would come to stare at the queers and the beatniks. But today there was nothing to see. The hippies were probably all asleep or getting themselves high in their pads.

Right in front of us, on both sides of the sidewalk, was a group of girls. They were just about old enough to pass for teeny-boppers. They must have spent a lot of time getting this whole trip organized. They probably took a bus from New Jersey, I figured, the way they were trying so hard to look as if they were born right here in the Village. Their parents would probably flip if they knew they were trying to make the Village scene, but I bet they wouldn't be half as scared as those little kids were. I could just imagine how they told each other that they will have to split into twos and threes so nobody would know they were together. They probably expected all sorts of fantastic adventures but nothing was happening to them.

Two of the girls seemed like leaders of the group. They were the only ones with long, ironed hair. The others had short hair and they probably all came from homes where short hair was considered sensible for the summer. The short-haired girls wore pants or shorts, and the two long-haired ones had mini-skirts on. I bet they thought they were real swingers. But I felt sorry for them. The Village looked so shoddy and nothing was happening and those kids would go back home to Jersey and they wouldn't have anything to tell their friends unless they lied.

We stopped at a crummy stand for a Coke although I wanted to go inside the Cafe Wha?. I watched Kevin looking around the street. He hadn't said anything for a long time and that worried me. He wasn't even being nonchalant about things. I mean he wasn't playing it cool or anything. He just looked eager and impatient. "Do you know anyone, any kid, who lives around here?" he suddenly asked me.

"No," I said.

I never felt lost or silly in New York before. When we lived in Manhattan, uptown on Madison Avenue and 92nd Street, Kevin and I used to bike over to the Village quite often. We felt we knew the Village then. We fooled around a lot. Once Kevin did this crazy bit from the movie "A Thousand Clowns." We were about where we stood now, and it was evening and the place was crawling with people and he started bawling me out for feeling sorry for myself just because I was a forty-year-old midget. You should have seen the people staring at us. I didn't break up or anything and then we got on our bikes and rode up Park Avenue screaming about volleyball practice and wanting to see a better grade of garbage. If you didn't see the movie you wouldn't know what I am talking about, but it was one of the better days in my life. But now I felt like a creep. The Village was like a place I'd never been in before. The sun would come out from behind the clouds and when it did the street looked even sadder than in the shade.

Just as I was finishing my Coke I caught sight of another group of teeny-boppers, even worse than the first one. Those girls had those high hairdos and their eyes were made up like Cleopatra's or something and they looked about three years behind the times, for God's sakes. Right behind them walked a couple of guys who were laughing at them and the girls tried real hard not to let on they heard any of their remarks.

If I hadn't been staring so hard he wouldn't have seen me. One of the two guys was from my school. I hated him. Not really, but I certainly didn't have any use for him. He was a tough sort of bully, about eighteen if he was a day, and he palled around with the seniors, a bunch of real degenerates.

"Hi, Jimmy baby. Making the scene?"

He stops in front of us and slaps me on the shoulder as if I was his real pal. His voice is so insulting and everything and he patronizes you as he breathes this bad breath right into your face. I wouldn't be surprised if he took some kind of pills to make his teeth stink so. He always puts down kids and pushes them around and even the teachers are scared of him. Our school doesn't have too many of those guys, but the group of seniors he hangs around with are really something. I bet they rob cars on weekends and maybe even kill people.

"Cat got your tongue, boy?" He makes a move to open my mouth and see for himself and I slap him away and he gets hold of my hand and squeezes it real hard. Kevin ordinarily would have flattened him by now but he just stands there as if nothing was happening.

"Let go, Chuck," I said.

"Say please," he says.

"Like hell I will," I say.

He still squeezes my hand and it's getting real sore and I look at Kevin and he is looking at the other guy.

"Came to get some grass?" Chuck says to me practically cracking my bones. "Or are you here to pick up some better grade of goodies?"

"Let go," I say.

"What's the matter, boy?"

"Let go of my hand, you queer," I say.

"You guys know where I can get some grass?" It was Kevin who had spoken. Chuck lets go of my hand and reaches into his pocket and brings out a little paper bag.

"Five will get you this," he says to Kevin.

Kevin gets his wallet out and hands him the money. "How about acid?" Kevin asks.

The other guy, who hadn't said a word, speaks up: "I got Methedrine, Dexamyl and amphetamine."

Just like that! As if he were some pharmacist or something.

"Nah," Kevin says. "I'd like to get hold of some acid. I don't go for that other stuff."

By now I'm really afraid that some cop will come up and we'll get busted. I mean here we were on the sidewalk, for God's sakes.

"Why don't you try the East Village?" Chuck says. He's talking to Kevin real nice. "For a buck I'll give you an address."

"O.K.," says Kevin and again he takes out his wallet, which, by the way, I sent him for Christmas together with the money, and hands over a bill and it must be my money too. Chuck takes out a piece of paper and a pen and scribbles down the address. "Just tell Leroy I sent you," he says.

And then the two of them flake off. I look after the creeps which is better than looking at Kevin. He's never done that to me before. He never let me down before. I mean he could have beat up on that creep Chuck.

As we walk east I feel very confused about everything. I don't talk to Kevin at all. Just a little while ago I felt guilty about him but now I feel ashamed for him and it's even worse. I mean when someone you respect and love lets you down like that it's like the end of the world. But the horrible thing is that he doesn't even *know* he let me down. I don't think he even saw that Chuck was hurting me. And as we walk I look at him from time to time and see that he keeps getting the piece of paper out of his pocket as if he couldn't remember the address that creep gave him. That was another thing about him, he used to have the most fantastic memory of anyone I ever knew.

I've been reading a lot of junk about the East Village, the hippies, the flower children and all that stuff and I thought the place would be really weird. But there we were, right in the middle of it all, on St. Marks and Second Avenue, and all I could see was a couple of photographers waiting. I mean nothing was happening and those guys with expensive equipment were just standing around. And not a hippie in sight. That practically broke me up.

"This is it, man," Kevin is saying as we come in front of a store of some kind. He tries the door but it's locked and it's dark inside. He looks down on his paper and up to the number over the door a couple of times and he knocks but there is nobody there. Inside this filthy window there are all sorts of signs and yellowing clippings and things and I can't make out what the store's about. We walk away from it, looking for the same number on the houses on both sides. But all there is is stores. So we go back and as we get to the door there is a lady opening it with a key and then bending down to get the mail that had been put in through the slot of the door. We wait until she straightens up and then Kevin says to her: "Does Leroy live here?"

She turns toward us and I thought she'd be jumpy or something, with us just standing behind her and all, but she's very cool and she says: "No, no one lives here. This is an office."

I really dig her accent. It's almost English, except I call it High American. It's so precise and beautiful and sharp, it seems to crackle actually. I know a couple of people who speak like that and they have real class and pretty great family backgrounds. But this dame doesn't look that classy or anything. She's wearing a tweedy sort of a suit that must be about a hundred years old and her hair is pretty miserable, thin and greyish and pulled back as if she didn't care to bother with it or anything.

"Come in," she says. She closes the door behind us and we're inside this narrow dark place and she goes over to the desk that stands in the back and pulls on a light chain. I look around but I still can't figure out what this place is all about. On the walls there are more yellowing clippings and signs and things like petitions or something. Anyway both of us are standing in front of her desk and it's piled high with old newspapers and some mail and stuff.

"Now, may I help you?" she says. She sat down on this rotten chair and she sounds like she's the President of the United States, for God's sakes. I mean she actually looks as if she knew that we were dependent on her for our very survival. And that's not far from the truth as far as Kevin is concerned. He looks real helpless.

"Maybe Leroy works here," he is saying. "I got this address . . ." He hands her the piece of paper and she takes it and looks at it.

"This is the correct address," she says, "but I'm afraid I don't know a Leroy."

Kevin just looks at her and she hands him back the piece of paper and by now I figure that this place is some kind of a headquarters for a campaign to preserve the neighborhood. There is a handbill right over the desk that says something about "the wanton destruction of old buildings." Those words are underlined in red. But it seems to me that whatever they wanted to do about the situation they gave up on it long ago. And maybe the lady is the only one who didn't give up. And I feel real great about her all of a sudden. I mean here she is, working for some forgotten lost cause and everything.

"Now, let's see." She has the phone book and is now looking through it. "We might possibly find your Leroy in the telephone book," she is saying. "Would that be his last or first name?"

"I think it's a first name," Kevin is saying.

"Then the phone book would be of no use," she says. "Would you have Leroy's family name by any chance?"

"No, I'm afraid not," Kevin says.

This is pretty fantastic, the two of them talking like that. She is so efficient but nothing is happening. How can it? She wouldn't be a pusher of LSD.

"If you told me," she is saying, "what this Leroy person does I might be of some help. I do know the tradespeople around these parts."

Kevin is now really embarrassed and doesn't say anything so I decide to tell her.

"He's got some acid," I say.

"Acid?" She repeats the word twice and tilts her head to the side and she looks like a bird. "Perhaps you should try the hardware store down the street."

That breaks me up. I mean you feed her information and she responds like an IBM machine. She would never be shocked by anything because she really didn't exist in this day and age. She is a passenger on the Mayflower and it is still at sea.

"Well, thank you very much," Kevin is saying, but I don't want to go yet.

"I am sorry I couldn't be of any help," she is saying and I want to say something to her but Kevin is pulling me.

At the door I turn back to look at her for the last time and she is looking down at the papers.

Out on the street there is a Great Dane walking alone and it's painted in stripes of different colors, blue and yellow and green and orange and violet, and a car is now parked in front of the store and it too is painted in this psychedelic way. I wonder what the lady would think of them, or whether she would see them at all. And I begin to laugh. It's really funny that she should be here, right in the neighborhood where it's all happening, where all those hippies are supposed to live. They are trying to escape reality using all those junky drugs. And she has really escaped it, by never having joined the world she was born into. I really wanted to talk about her to Kevin.

"Hey, wasn't she something?" I say for a start.

"You sure were dumb telling her about acid," he says, sounding real disgusted with me.

"Don't you get it? Even if I had said to her that we came for LSD she wouldn't know what we were talking about. Or maybe she'd ask how you spell it so she could look it up in the phone book." It's funny I run her down because I actually admire her and everything, especially for fighting for that lost, forgotten cause. But Kevin isn't interested in her at all. So I ask him where we're going.

"I don't know," he says. "Why don't you beat it home?"

"Because I don't want to."

"What is it called? Something Square, where it's like the center of the whole hippie deal?"

"Tompkins Square," I say.

As we walked toward Tompkins Square I was beginning to feel much better. By now I was pretty sure that Kevin wouldn't find any LSD and that soon he'd get disgusted with looking for it and I could talk him into a movie.

Old St. Mark's looked really stupid. Some of those crummy old houses were being remodeled, and where there used to be all those Polish and Jewish stores they now had these phony boutiques. They were everywhere and not a customer in sight. That really killed me. All that publicity about the East Village, it was so much hogwash. The old place wasn't swinging at all. It was dead.

When we finally got to Tompkins Square I thought we were going to see some action. There were about a dozen policemen around. But they were just standing, doing nothing, like those photographers. And in the park there were no hippies. Just the old Polish ladies, in their babushkas sunning themselves and gossiping away, and the old gents playing chess and reading newspapers. Just like years ago. Just as if nothing at all was happening.

"Let's go to a flick," I said to Kevin. "Nothing's going on here." But he just kept on walking. I could tell he was really furious by now. But he's stubborn and he wouldn't give up that easy.

In the middle of the square, where there is this sort of an open stage, there were a few long-haired cats and even a guitar-player or two, but for all the noise they were making you might as well have been at the Radio City Music Hall at 7 A.M. Kevin gives them a once-over but decides to keep walking and finally we turn back.

I was beginning to whistle, I was feeling that great, when all of a sudden Kevin points to this guy who's walking in front of us.

"I bet he'd know."

"Know what?"

"I bet he'd know where I could get hold of some acid."

The guy in front looks real strange, like a puppet or something. He sort of swings through the air. Everything he's got is moving, his feet, arms, head, hands. And he walks fast. We don't seem to be gaining on him although we're hurrying. He stops at the drinking fountain and Kevin walks up to him. I stay behind, because I'm ashamed as hell. What the hell is my genius brother doing chasing after some nutty-looking guy like that?

I don't claim to understand much of what goes on in the world or, for that matter, what goes on with me. All I know is that we were supposed to be created in God's image which wouldn't allow us to act or feel like jackasses. Well, I acted and felt like one. And it made me angry as hell.

"What about beating it home," Kevin says, coming up to me. "You don't have to hang around."

"Where you going?" I ask him.

"With this guy to his pad."

"I'm coming with you," I say.

"Come on, beat it," Kevin says under his breath.

"I'm coming with you," I say again.

The weird guy is just standing looking at us. He is smiling and it makes his face look real funny because a piece of his front tooth is missing, and right over it, his upper lip is sewed up. He is no more than eighteen, I figure, but he's got a fairly heavy beard on him. His hair isn't all that long, though, and he's wearing beat-up jeans and a dirty shirt but no jewelry or anything like that. He doesn't look like a hippie, and he's not a bad-looking guy for a guy with a knocked-out tooth.

"Take him along," the hippie guy says to Kevin. Kevin doesn't say anything. He just gives me a dirty look and starts walking and I trail behind them. It's funny to see them walking side by side but I don't feel like laughing. I'm really mad. I mean we were supposed to have a great summer and everything and here I'm acting like a jackass and Kevin hates having me around.

"How long have you been living here?" Kevin is asking the guy. I guess he's trying to be sociable but I bet all he's thinking of is that junk he's going to get.

"I came here last April," the guy says.

"Where from?"

"Upstate New York."

"You figure on going back home?"

"In September. I'm going back to finish school."

"What do you live on here?"

"Mostly bumming," the guy says. I can't see his face but I just know he's smiling. He takes out some money from his pocket and shows it to Kevin. "I got over six dollars today."

"You mean you panhandled it?"

"I got more but I gave some to a bum. They're having a tough time now. With all of us bumming they're not doing as well as they used to. It's easier for us to get money than for them."

What surprised me even more than the fact that the

guy is begging around the streets and then sharing the money with bums, was that he didn't talk like I thought a hippie would. So I moved over to his side and asked him if he was on anything.

"I used to smoke grass," he says. I glanced over at Kevin and he's glaring at me.

"But you don't any more?" I ask him.

"No. I don't need to. Besides I dig being with people and when I was on grass I always wanted to split and be alone."

He makes me feel better and I like him all of a sudden. He could make a difference to Kevin. He could tell him what I couldn't. About how horrible all those habits are.

"All that stuff," I say, "is junk, isn't it? I mean, it's dangerous to fool around with, isn't it?"

"I don't know about that," the guy says. "All I know is it wasn't doing me any good."

"But your friends? How about them? Do they take any stuff?"

"Most do," he says.

"What happens to them?"

"Some can take it, some can't."

"Those who can't, what happens to them?"

"They freak out."

By now we're in front of a real lousy-looking house. The bricks were painted once and the paint is peeling all over the place and the rusty fire escape is hanging all crooked and the stoop steps are all chewed up. I'm dying to ask the guy all sorts of questions, not only for Kevin's benefit, but because I'm curious about him. I mean how did he get his lip busted? And how come he goes around giving money to the bums and what does he do with himself when he's not bumming, and what does his family think about him living in the East

Village? But we're going up the stairs in a single file and he's ahead of Kevin and me. As usual I'm bringing up the rear.

The staircase is pretty dark. The only light comes from two frosted-glass doors on each landing. And it stinks. It really does. There is a toilet on each landing, between the two apartments, and paper bags with garbage are standing around, some of them spilling over.

The guy doesn't have to use a key or anything because the door isn't locked. I guess I expected him to live here alone, but as we came in, the first thing I saw were a lot of mattresses on the floor and about five guys and two girls sitting on them. And the next thing I saw was the back of this girl. She is taking a bath, for God's sakes! She is all naked, I swear, and she's not sitting in a regular bathtub but in a sort of a large laundry sink.

"Close the door," she says. "There is a draft on my back."

Just like that! She doesn't look to see who's come in or anything like that, just yells about the draft, and there she is scrubbing away, and right in the next room, a room without even a door or anything, there is this bunch of guys.

Well, I don't look at her and I'm actually trying to forget that I ever saw her. I follow the guy with the busted lip and Kevin to the room with all those mattresses and nobody is saying anything. I mean nobody bothers about us coming in. And they don't seem even aware that the girl is taking a bath right in front of them, for God's sakes!

The next room we go into looks a little better. I mean the other one had only those dirty mattresses and nothing else. But in here there is a folding cot and a guy is asleep on it and there is a dresser with a couple of drawers missing. There is nothing else there, except for a couple of paperback books and a beat-up poster for some off-Broadway play. That's on the wall all right, except it's hanging upside down.

I don't know what to think about this place. I mean I expected a hippie pad to have a lot of music from a hi-fi, and hippies playing guitars and stuff like posters on the walls but there is nothing like that around. It's as if anything that you could buy or pawn wasn't allowed here. It looks as if whoever lives here doesn't even need things like chairs. And there are no lamps or anything like bulbs, so they probably don't even use electricity. And besides that laundry sink, I didn't notice any kitchen things. I mean there wasn't anything like an icebox or a stove. And there are no doors separating those three rooms, not even a curtain. It's just one miserable railroad flat with very little daylight coming through the dirty windows that give out on a shaft.

The guy who brought us is trying to wake up the guy who is on the cot but he keeps on sleeping, unless he's dead or passed out.

"He was on speed and he's fallen out," the guy is saying as if he wanted to explain this to us. "Maybe someone in the other room has some acid." He smiles at us and adds, "This is one groovy crash pad. If you ever need a place, you can stay here."

"Thanks," Kevin says and I don't say anything. He's very generous and all and I like that all right, except what the hell is he offering us?

We're back in the middle room and there is still nothing being said in there. But now I guess they must all be high on pot and don't need to talk. And besides there is a strange smell around this place that I hadn't noticed, maybe because the girl shook me up so much. There is something burning in the middle of the floor and I figure it must be incense, because I don't smell pot, just this sort of perfumey stuff. Anyway, they're just sitting around and no one is looking at the girl. She's still in that tub and I can't take my eyes off her. I mean how many times does a guy see a thing like that in his lifetime?

"Anyone got any acid?" our guy asks.

A couple of the guys look toward him and now I notice that nobody is older than twenty, and the girls look much younger. Anyway, besides those two guys who looked up, the others don't seem to even know we're there. And the two guys look as if they hadn't heard the question. But just as I was going to pull at Kevin's sleeve and tell him we ought to leave, this older guy, with a red beard and long hair, who had his head way back against the wall, speaks up:

"You can have my cap," he says. He says it real slow and doesn't look at us but at the ceiling, and he doesn't make a move and it's sort of strange because I think I just imagined him speaking. I mean I feel real queer, like when I was high on pot yesterday.

"I wouldn't want to take it away from you if it's the only one you've got," Kevin says.

"It's all right," the guy says and he still doesn't look at anything except the ceiling.

"Will you take five dollars for it?" Kevin says taking out his wallet again.

"Forget the bread," the guy says. He hadn't moved an inch in all that time.

"Where is it, man?" the guy who brought us asks. The guy must have gone back to whatever dreamland he was in before because he doesn't answer and now his eyes are closed.

"It's in the kitchen. Top shelf," one of the girls says and she sort of waves her hand in that direction. It's real queer the way they talk and act, so slowly and dream-like as if they had all the time in the world to do nothing.

So we go back to the kitchen and I move to the door trying not to look at the girl in the tub, but she turns her head and sees me and says: "Hi!"

I'm so embarrassed I don't say anything back and she keeps looking at me and smiles and then says: "Where did you come from?" But she doesn't wait for me to answer and turns her face away and starts to hum to herself as she goes back to washing.

I just can't get over that. Maybe I'm a sex maniac or something but that really makes me forget everything else. I mean I'm no longer thinking of Kevin and what we've come here for or anything else. I'm just thinking how marvelous and strange that girl is and how much I'd like to get to know her and how stupid I feel.

The guy who brought us grabs a few empty soda bottles and comes downstairs with us.

"Do all those people live there?" I ask him. What I really want to know is the girl's name but I don't ask him that.

"Sometimes there are more, and sometimes there are less of them," he says. "But I've only been here for a month."

"What do those guys live on?" Kevin asks.

"Same as me. Just on what we can bum."

"Do the girls bum too?" I asked trying not to sound too curious.

"Sure," the guy said and smiled. "We all take turns. This week it's my turn."

"What were they all doing in that room?" I ask.

"Grooving," he says and smiles again. We're at the

front door by now and he says good-bye to us.

"I'm grocery shopping this week," he says.

"I've got to give you some money," Kevin says and starts taking out his wallet.

"No, that's O.K.," the guy says and walks away.

We begin to go in the opposite direction, toward Astor Place. I'm thinking about the girl. I mean I couldn't really describe her. She had hair that was sort of coiled on top of her head, light brown, I think. And she didn't have any lipstick or anything on her face or eyes and I think she had a pretty nice smile. I really would have liked to have talked to her, ask her what makes her want to live in a place like that. She wasn't like the others at all. She was aware that we were there, for crying out loud. She wasn't just goofing. She was doing something. Something practical. I just can't believe that she takes pot or anything like acid. I know she doesn't. I really don't know what the hell she was doing there. Maybe it's her apartment. No, I guess it can't be. Her place would be nice and clean and would have all sorts of nice things in it. Maybe she just came there to take a bath or something.

Anyway that's what I was thinking about as we walk down the street. I was even figuring that I could talk Kevin into coming back to that pad sometime soon. If we did I'd talk to the girl. I'd ask her what she was doing there. If she ran away from home and didn't have any money and didn't want to go back home I could maybe talk her into coming and staying with us. Mom wouldn't mind. She'd like her, and we have this guest room with a regular bath and all, and our place would be really good for her. I just hate to see her in that horrible pad with those strange people. And I bet that if I asked her to come and stay with us she wouldn't take it the wrong way or anything. She's much older than I am, maybe even older than Kevin, so she wouldn't think I was trying to make out with her or anything.

"Those were nice guys," Kevin is saying. "They really share things. They really do. That's what's so nice about them. They don't care about things, possessions I mean. Like that guy who gave away the money he bummed. I really dig that. But I couldn't be like them."

"I hope not," I say.

"I wish I could, but I can't be like them," Kevin says.

"You mean you wouldn't mind living like them?" I ask.

"You didn't dig that place at all, did you?" he asks me.

"I sure didn't," I say. "What were they all doing? What did the guy mean, grooving?"

"Having fun. They were stoned," Kevin says.

"But not that girl," I say.

"Which one?"

"Which one?" I yell. "The one who was washing herself in the tub!"

"In where?"

He was either putting me on or he didn't even notice her.

"Didn't you see her?" I ask him.

"I guess not," he says and I know he isn't putting me on and it makes me really mad. I mean how far gone was he not to even notice a thing like that?

"You got that stupid junk," I say to him. "Is that all you can think about, taking that stuff? Is that all?"

"I will take it when I'm ready," he says.

"You mean you're not going to take it right away?"

"No. I'll wait and see."

I guess I'd expected him to take the stuff right away. I

don't know whether I wanted him to get it over with or what. But I was both relieved and disappointed. Now I hope maybe he won't take it. Maybe something will happen and he won't want to take it at all.

WEDNESDAY, JUNE 14

Kevin slept late again today and I went into his room twice trying to find where he stashed that stuff. I didn't even know what to look for or anything. All I could remember was that the guy referred to it as a "cap" and I thought that LSD came in a sugar cube. Anyway I couldn't find it. And I'm still worried about it just being there in his room. But I've finally decided that if I don't remind him of it he might forget it. Fat chance!

By late afternoon I got to talk to him alone.

"Those friends of yours in Chicago," I said, "the ones who take that awful junk. How often do they do it?"

"You mean acid?"

"Yeah."

"Not often," he said. "Those who are really on it don't take it more than once a month, twice at most. It takes a hell of a lot out of you. I mean it's a pretty tremendous experience."

"Bigger than grass?"

"Man, grass is nothing in comparison!"

"You're kidding!"

I couldn't believe it! I mean ever since I smoked that

junk I've felt sort of queer and light-headed as if I was still feeling its effects.

"Acid isn't dangerous like speed," he said.

"Speed? What's that?"

"Methedrine."

"What does it do to you?"

"If you're really on it, it will kill you after a while."

"What the hell would anyone want to fool around with things like that for?" I asked him, sort of shouting.

"Some people have real hang-ups and they try anything so they won't feel up tight all the time."

"Hell, they should be locked up!" I really shouted then.

"Instead people make such a big fuss over them."

"Who does?"

"Everybody! Magazines and TV . . ."

"The Establishment is making money out of them. That has nothing to do with what they're about. They're just doing their own thing."

"And what's that? Killing themselves with drugs?"

"The drug scene is not what I'm talking about."

"Well, that's what I'm talking about!"

"Then you better be talking to yourself."

He got off the bed and started to leave the room. But I stopped him.

"O.K., I'll leave the junk out," I said, and he sat down again and gave me this half smile. I was still mad, but I tried not to show it. "So what's great about the hippies?" I asked.

He takes hold of a news magazine which he had been reading before I came into the room and looks through it.

"I'm only for them," he says, "because the wrong people are against them." He finds the page he wants and begins to read: "For those of you who don't know what a hippie is, he's a fellow who has hair like

Tarzan, who walks like Jane, and who smells like Cheetah." He throws the magazine across the room and I watch it sail until it crashes against the wall.

"Yeah, that's pretty stupid. Who said it?"

"The governor of California," he says.

"Do you think a guy like that could be President?"

"Sure, he's got power, hasn't he?"

"But—"

He doesn't let me finish. He looks really fed up now. "Hell, don't you get it?" he says. "It's not only me who's got to worry about the circles. The whole world is lousy with dead ends. O.K., let's take the hippies again. At first, when all this hippie stuff started, they seemed to me like the early Christians. They knew something the rest of us didn't. Boy, did they seem great! I figured they didn't wash because they wanted to show that the outside dirt doesn't matter, but inside dirt does. And they didn't give a damn about material things, such as jobs and possessions, because they didn't want to be burdened with unnecessary garbage. And they talked about love as if they really understood what Christ was all about. But then what happened? The Establishment moves in. It starts by taking notice of them, and ends up by making money off them. You want to be poor and live like Saint Francis, and what happens? The exploiters take your photograph, sell the kind of clothes you wear, put a neon sign over your pad and charge admission to the tourists who want to see what a psychedelic freak looks like. And you become a freak, or the scene begins to attract idiots. So by now it's all different. And that's what I am saying to you—nothing good and fine can exist in this rotten world for very long."

"But how can the world get any better if the good people cop out?"

"Man, it's too late for the world to get better. It's so rotten that you've just got to withdraw from it."

"I don't buy that," I shout at him. "It's a great world and no punky hippie dropout failure is going to tell me otherwise!"

"I'm telling it to you. And I'm no hippie."

"I don't buy it from you either!"

He laughed then, the frightening laugh that I hate so much, and when he was through laughing he said: "Wouldn't that be a groove? The world right and only me wrong?" And for a moment, a very short moment, like a split second, he looked worried sick.

But then he shook his head, jumped off the bed and said: "O.K., let me beat the stuffing out of you on a tennis court. I can still do that much. Ready?"

He grabbed his racket and smacked my bottom with it, and it was like old times, and I laughed too and ran out of his room and got my tennis stuff and didn't have time to worry about all the things he had said. Until now, when I stop to think about them.

I almost beat him. I came real close but he ended up taking each set 7-5, 7-5, 7-5.

THURSDAY, JUNE 15

Last night we watched a couple of late movies on television. I was still asleep when Kevin came into my room around ten this morning and woke me up.

"Want to go to the library with me?"

"Sure," I said. "I ought to check out some books on my reading list."

On the way over I asked him what he wanted from the library.

"A couple of books on biorhythm," he said.

"On what?"

"Biorhythm. It's sort of a scientific way of charting cycles."

"What cycles?"

"Our cycles, for Christ's sakes!"

After a little while he cooled down and tried to explain it to me.

"We're all supposed to have cycles. Mostly three— physical, intellectual and emotional. Anyway, at different times we get what they call critical days and low days and high days."

"What are you interested in junk like that for?" I asked him. "Isn't it like horoscopes or something?"

"No, it's more scientific. I mean they figured it out from watching nature and animals. They use biorhythm a lot in Europe, especially in Switzerland."

"What for? There is nothing happening in Switzerland. It's about the deadest country there is."

"I don't know what the hell they use it for," he says and he's mad again. I don't know what makes him so touchy but I apologize and I feel bad that I was putting the thing down without knowing anything about it.

"What does it do anyway? How does it work?" He doesn't answer me, so I try again. "I'm sorry," I say. "I didn't mean to sound so smart-alecky. How about this thing . . . bio, what?"

"Biorhythm," he says.

"Yeah, tell me about it."

"I told you about it."

"What do you want to do with it?" I ask him. And again he doesn't answer. "Hey, tell me," I say. "I really want to know. Honest."

"Nothing," he says. "Forget it."

"Oh, come on. I'm really interested. I even sneak a look at my horoscope in the paper. I think I'd believe in it and everything."

"I'll get some books on it and then we can make our charts," he says. It's all right now. He isn't mad at me so I stop bugging him with the questions.

Back home we read the books together. It's sort of fascinating, in a dumb way, and I can see it would really be a help to people, to get them organized. I mean if you were a writer or something you could use your chart to see how creative you are on certain days. For the average guy the whole method can explain why he's having a bad day or a good day. I intend to use my chart for my tennis. I mean I won't play at all on my low days and play all day on my high days.

It took us about three hours to go through the books and make our charts. After I made mine up I wanted to see Kevin's but he didn't want to show it to me. He was making another chart for last May.

"What do you want to know about last May for?" I ask him. He is really involved in this chart thing.

"I want to see something," he says. I wait for him to finish. When he does he looks up and says, "I knew it!" He doesn't say it to me, actually. He just says it. So I asked him what he knew.

"On May 11th I had a triple critical day," he says. "A real honest-to-God triple whammy." He explains it. "That means that on that day my physical, emotional and intellectual capacities were in a state of flux. All of them at once."

"What happened on that day?" I ask him.

"I had the bad trip," he says.

All of a sudden I know what he wants to make the chart for. And now he knows that I know so he smiles at me and shows me the chart for this month.

"Look at it," he says. "On Saturday I'll have all three lines at their peak high."

I didn't even dare ask him if he intends to take LSD on that day. I am sure he does but I don't want to know it. I am so scared that I feel the fear in my guts. I am so scared I can't even try to talk him out of it. I just sit there and stare at my feet. It's that bad. I can't even look at him. After a while he speaks to me and all I can hear is this buzzing in my head and his words coming at me from a long way off.

"I'm going to blow mom and dad to a matinee and dinner in town this Saturday," he is saying. "I'm going to go and get the tickets and make a reservation. How about Sardi's? I think they'd like to go to Sardi's. Want to come with me and get the tickets?"

"No," I say.

"O.K.," he says. And he leaves the room.

After he left I began to feel real sick. I had to go to the bathroom and everything. And then I lay down on my bed and wanted to die. I made myself get up after a while and I wrote everything down. And now I feel better. I mean if that biorhythm has some validity then Saturday would be the best day for him to take the junk. And he is going to take it anyway. But to make sure that nothing will happen to him, I will go to Mass tomorrow and Saturday morning anyway.

It's been years since I went to Mass on a weekday. The closest church to us is about twenty blocks away and I had to get up earlier than I ever do, to make the seven o'clock Mass. I didn't want anyone to know, and I figured on coming back before they woke up.

It was sort of surprising to me to see so many people at Mass. When I was a small kid and went to a parochial school in Manhattan I'd go to church on weekdays sometimes and there were only a few old ladies there and maybe a bum sleeping in a pew. But today it all seemed so different. The place was almost half full and not with little old ladies either. There were mostly working people, both men and women but women still outnumbering the men seven to one or something like that. I didn't actually count, of course, but I looked around.

There was one man there, maybe in his fifties, who looked to me as if he might have had a heart attack recently. I mean he looked as if he was feeling his way around, as if he wasn't trusting himself too much yet. I imagined all sorts of things about him, that he had lost his job, that his wife had left him, that he couldn't find work and had a mortgage on the house to pay. I really felt for him. It's strange because middle-aged people don't interest me in the least. The thing that got me about him was that he probably had no one to run to. Or maybe he did. Maybe he had God. But that's not enough if you're living among people.

Anyway, it was pretty close to Communion time before

I started praying for Kevin. I explained the whole deal to God, about my not being able to help or anything, and about how scared I was for him. I asked God to watch over him and to make it clear to him that the stuff was no good for him.

But as I left the church I realized that it was pretty cheap of me to run for help to God like that. I have this friend Milton who is Jewish, who thinks that it's not fair to bug God with problems. "Either God loves you and watches over you or He doesn't," he once told me. "If you think He doesn't you're an atheist. If you know He does then He can do it without you reminding Him."

But I can't be like Milton. I wish I could have the kind of relationship with God he has, but I don't. I wish I could talk back to God like he does. Once we went out together to practice tennis. We're doubles partners and we practice a lot together, especially just before a tournament. And just as we got to the courts it started to rain. So Milton looks up, clenches his fists and shouts: "Hey, God, what do you think you're doing? Cut it out, will ya? I know you can make rain. But hold it off today."

Another time, in school, he slammed the desk top on his hand. We were being kept after school for ditching a class and playing tennis instead. Well, that time, instead of yelling or anything, he looks up and says, "Lay off me, God. Go and pick on someone else for a change."

I'd give anything to be like that with God, but I can't. Anyway, I had a pretty good thing going for a while, but now it's not the same. It's as if by growing up I had to give up the way I felt about Him when I was a kid. And I don't like giving up anything any more than I like things to change. But I haven't begun to worry about all this, not yet. If it gets worse I probably will.

Anyway all I'm worried about now is that stuff Kevin plans to take and what it might do to him. So I plan to go to Mass again tomorrow morning and try to pray properly.

This afternoon Kevin and I played tennis for about five hours. He beat me very badly. I barely managed to get three games in six sets. He laughed a lot during all that time, and kidded around, making a couple of fantastic shots with his racket held behind his back. And at the end of it, as we walked towards the clubhouse, he slapped me on the back and said:

"You see, it works."

"What?"

"The biorhythm stuff. I played so well because all my faculties are near the perfect high." And then he laughed again. "Wait until tomorrow."

"Let's play tomorrow," I said very fast.

"No," he said. "I'll be busy."

"Come on, let's play tomorrow," I said, trying to sound casual as hell and all the time scared of what he'd be doing tomorrow.

"O.K.," he says. "We'll play in the morning."

"I'll beat you."

"Want to bet?"

"How much?" I ask him.

"Forget it, shrimp. Nobody's beating me tomorrow." And then he laughed. "Tomorrow I beat the world."

It's about one o'clock and mom and dad are about to leave. I wish I could stop them from going. I'm so scared that I am actually sweating. It was no good at Mass. I couldn't pray at all. I really tried. I even tried to reach that third-rater of an angel who helped me fight for Kevin when I was high. But I couldn't reach him. And then I got real depressed. I was in church and I wished I was dead. And that made the whole thing like a sacrilege.

When I got back from Mass, Kevin was having breakfast by himself. Mom and dad were still asleep.

"Where have you been?" he asked.

His eyes were very bright and his hands shook when he lifted the coffee cup. I didn't want to tell him and I didn't feel like lying so I didn't answer him and got busy fixing breakfast. We didn't speak at all, and then when I was doing the dishes Kevin said to hurry up so we could get the tennis over with.

"If you don't want to play you don't have to, you know," I said.

"Cut it out," he said. "Let's go."

We played two sets. I beat him 6–3, 6–2, and even the games he got I actually tried to lose. And besides, I could barely concentrate myself. The whole thing was awful. I think he was worried sick. I mean according to his chart he should have been on the very top of his form. He tried to joke about it, but he didn't do a good job. And all I could think of is that maybe now he will realize that he shouldn't take that junk after all. But I didn't say anything. I tried to act as if I wasn't worried about a thing, as if all that mattered was the fact that I beat him. I tried to make a big deal out of that but I did a bad job of it too.

If only mom and dad weren't going away everything would be all right. But they are. They're calling good-bye right now. And I can hear the car back out of the garage and I want to yell to them not to go. But they were so excited last night about seeing the play. It's called "You Know I Can't Hear You When the Water's Running," and they had wanted to see it but never got around to writing for tickets. Anyway, they made a real fuss over Kevin getting them the tickets and arranging their whole day. I had to leave the room, I just couldn't stand it. They probably won't be back before ten tonight. They're planning to act like a couple of tourists and take a boat ride around Manhattan before having dinner at Sardi's.

They're wonderful parents and everything and I really love them and they don't even bug me much, but why can't they see that there is something terribly wrong with Kevin? Why can't they tell?

I better get the hell out of my room and see what Kevin's up to. I don't want to leave him alone. Maybe I will try to talk him out of taking the stuff.

It was so terrible. All of it, every moment of it. And now he is gone. They've taken him away.

God, it's all my fault. I could have stopped it from happening. I could at least have tried. I deserve to be killed.

But what the hell am I doing thinking of myself again? I must write down everything that happened. It might be of some use to the doctors at Sweetmountain, the private hospital where they took Kevin. Mom and dad thought it would be important, if I wrote everything down just as it happened.

They read the notebook. They found it in my room when they got home. I was already asleep, knocked out by some stuff the doctor gave me. Anyway, mom and dad were crying all over the notebook when I woke up. We talked then. They're really shook up by what happened, but even more, they can't forgive themselves for not knowing what was going on. I tried to explain to them that parents never know anything about their own kids, that's sort of natural, but they don't go for that. They blame themselves, and it's not their fault. It's mostly my fault. I shouldn't have written the stuff about them.

It's so hard to write about what happened. It was worse than any nightmare.

Kevin was in his room, sitting on his bed. He didn't have to tell me he had already taken the stuff. I knew it.

"I want it to be different," he said to me. "I don't want a good trip or a bad trip. I want to get some insights into myself. I need them. I need to know what is wrong with me." He smiled sort of shakily. "Don't worry, shrimp. Everything will be all right. It's got to be. I have it planned this way."

"How long before you . . . before you feel anything?" I asked him.

"Forty minutes or so, maybe less, a half hour."

"What if anything . . ."

"Goes wrong?"

"Yes."

"Nothing will."

"But if it does, what do I do?"

"Stick by me."

"I will," I said. "I will do that. But if you need help . . ."

"Don't talk like that! I'm trying hard not to think that . . ."

He gets off his bed and goes to the window. He has his back to me as he talks. "Some people think that all of it has to do with the right vibrations. Maybe they're right. Don't go against me. Just ride with me. Pull for me. Will you do that?"

"Sure," I say.

He doesn't turn toward me, and his back looks very tense through the shirt.

"The mind is a very tricky thing," he says. "And when you upset its balance you might find gold or you might find . . ." Again he doesn't finish the sentence. "You see, I've got to do it for myself. Finding out. I can't wait any longer. That's why I took acid this time. To make it come to me. I'm going to make my mind my servant. And I'll be the explorer. It will be all good." He turns around then and he actually looks happy. It's the first time that he's looked that way since he came back. "Just stick by me. I need you around. And don't get frightened, no matter what. Promise?"

"I promise," I say. But I am more frightened than ever. And I don't want to be. I keep thinking that if I feel frightened it will affect him, so I try very hard not to be scared. But the fear is there, deep down, and I can't do anything about it.

Kevin goes back to his bed and sits on it and looks at me.

"You're part of it all," he says. "You and mom and dad. Somewhere, something didn't go right. And I don't know what it is or where it is or how I can cope with it." He reaches out and messes up my hair. "No matter what happens," he says and smiles, "I want you to know that I care for you. But I'll be alone soon and even though you'll be with me I'll be all alone. That's how it is. It's looking inward and you won't be part of it. But remember that I'll need you. No matter how it is with me I want you around."

I don't say anything because he knows that I understand. I just nod my head. I also know something else. He would like to tell me what I should do if things go wrong. But he doesn't dare. He doesn't want to put any jinx on it. He is scared, though, I know. But he fights it. And there we are, both of us, just sitting in his room, trying to fight fear without letting each other know. And there is something else. We love each other. And nothing can change that, no matter what happens. I want to tell him but he beats me to it.

"We have a good thing going between us," he says. "It's strong and good and nothing will happen to that. Remember that much. Nothing will ever destroy that."

"I know," I say.

"O.K., shrimp," he says and gets up again and this time he goes to the door and holds it open for me.

"Now you leave me alone for a little while."

"But you wanted me to stay!"

"Just for a little while. Give me five minutes to be alone."

"But why?"

"I want to . . ." He hesitates and then blurts it out and I know he's embarrassed. "I'd just like . . . to pray for a while."

I go out of his room and hear the door close and wonder if he had locked it. That's all I try to keep thinking about. I figure that if he locked it I'd be able to jimmy up his window from the outside. I've done that before. I think about the stupid door because I don't want to think about what is happening inside of him, in those parts where I don't belong, where I'll never be, the parts that nobody knows about except him.

I'll try as best as I can to keep my own feelings out of this because what I felt is of no use to anyone. All that matters is getting Kevin back.

By then it was ten to two. Mom and dad left around one thirty and Kevin went to his room as they were leaving. If he had taken the LSD before, I wouldn't know how much time had passed, but if he waited until they left, then twenty minutes had gone by. So I go back and knock on his door. He doesn't answer and I try the knob. It isn't locked.

At first I don't see him in the room and I figure he must be in the bathroom. But as I close the door behind me I see him. He is wedged in the corner, sitting on the floor, his whole body hunched up as if he wanted to shrink right out of existence. He looks so small, so strangely small, that I don't notice his eyes right away. They are wild with terror.

"What is it?" I shout.

He is looking straight ahead but I know he can't see me. Both of his hands are protecting his throat and his elbows are jammed against his chest. Suddenly his right arm shoots out and he is trying to push something away with it. His left hand is pushing too, but it stays near his throat. He is struggling against something invisible that is trying to choke him. It is horrible to see him struggle like that.

"It's all right," I say. "I'm here now."

Gently I take hold of his right hand. It feels sweaty and cold. He stopped fighting the minute I touched him and he is all limp as I lift him up and lead him to a chair, but his eyes are still wild with fright, staring straight ahead. His left hand is still protecting his throat. I make him sit down on the chair and kneel beside him.

"There are no more circles," I say. "They won't come back."

I take his left hand away from his throat and hold both his hands in mine and I try to warm them by breathing on them. He looks at me, but I don't think he knows who I am. Then he looks away from me and around the room and slowly up towards the ceiling. And then he begins to shake all over.

"They are not there either," I say. I know he sees the circles up there, near the ceiling somewhere. "They won't come back. They'll never come back again."

I wasn't sure that he heard me, or even if I had been right about the circles, but then he whispers something. Leaning close to him I can barely make out: "They will choke me." He is still looking up, but he had finally spoken, and I had been afraid he'd never say anything to me.

"There are no circles," I repeat very slowly. "They don't really exist. You think they're there, but they aren't. Look at me. I can prove it to you."

I shake him by the shoulders and then try to lower his head but I can't manage. His eyes are on the ceiling as if they are connected to it. And he looks blind.

I kept thinking that if he could hear my voice, if the sound of it penetrated to him, he'd be all right. I actually believed that if I kept talking I could keep those circles at bay.

"I never told you about this new English teacher I have," I said. I kept holding on to his hands so that they wouldn't shoot upwards, but he pulls loose and stretches them toward the ceiling. His fingers are spread so wide I think they'll break. I can't bear to see him like that so I turn away but I don't stop talking. I talk about stupid things, especially my school. I keep wishing there was a phone extension in Kevin's room. I could call the police or our doctor or granddad. But there is no phone and one thing I know is that I should not leave him, not even for a second.

Outside some kids begin to play baseball and I become aware of other sounds too. The cars passing by, a lawn mower, and the bells on a Good Humor truck. And all those noises are a terrific comfort, because I must have thought, ever since I came to his room, that we were all alone in the world. If it hadn't been for those noises, I would have gone stark raving mad. It will all be over soon, I think. And I keep talking.

For over an hour I talked to him. When I was through with school, I started on the tennis tournaments, the books I've been reading, what was said and who said it at the Wigwam. And he never moved. His hands kept holding back the terror, his eyes were still glued to the ceiling.

Then suddenly he screamed out and grabbed at his throat and he was on the floor, thrashing, grabbing at the air around his neck, pushing away.

I don't know what made me do it. Instinct, maybe, or possibly the idea came from God. I couldn't bear to see his agony and I threw myself on the floor and began to beat my hands against whatever it was that he fought against. And he stopped thrashing around and got up and shouted at me:

"You got rid of them! You destroyed the circles!" He looked all around the room and upwards toward the ceiling and then at me.

"They're gone!" he said, and repeated those words again and again with wonder in his voice.

I began to laugh and cry at the same time and I think

he was laughing and crying with me. I put my arms around him. I could feel his sweat soaking into my shirt.

"It's all right," I kept saying. "It's all over now." After a while he broke away and ran to the bathroom. I followed him. He was standing in front of the mirror but he was not looking at himself.

"I wanted to see my neck, where they were," he whispered. "But I'm afraid they're still around me."

"No, they're gone for good," I assured him. "Look at yourself."

But he wouldn't or he couldn't.

"I'm afraid," he said and repeated it over and over again, standing in front of that mirror not daring to look at himself.

"Don't be afraid," I told him. "Look at yourself. There is nothing near your neck. Prove it to yourself."

"I can't," he said. "I'll see them."

"Then don't look, but believe me, they're gone."

He turned toward me then.

"You destroyed them," he said. "How did you do that?" It was the first time since I came to his room that he seemed almost normal.

"I don't know how I did it," I said. "But I can do it again. And the circles know that. They won't bother you again."

After that he tried again to look in the mirror. He really tried, but he just couldn't. And then he noticed the razor on the edge of the washbasin and he picked it up and kept turning it over and over, and I had to take it away from him because I was afraid he'd cut himself.

"Let's go to the living room," I said taking him by the hand. "Let's watch the ball game on television."

He let me lead him. He seemed to have trouble

walking but I held on to him. He stumbled a few times but didn't fall. I made him sit down on the sofa and went to turn the set on.

"What is that sound?" he asked.

I couldn't hear anything but the grandfather's clock. It sounded quite loud because there was no other noise in the room.

"You mean the ticking?" I asked.

"The explosions," he said. "Where do the explosions come from?"

He kept looking at the clock.

"It's just that old clock," I said.

The picture and the sound came on the television and I had to turn it down and make it less bright because it seemed to hurt both his eyes and his ears. He would put his hands over his eyes and then remove them and put them over his ears and sit with his eyes closed, and then he would open them again only to hide them from the television glare. He didn't seem terrified any more. I could have called a doctor then but I was sure the worst was over. I even began to watch the game and got excited over a double play followed by a real beautiful catch off the fence. And during a commercial I left him and went to the kitchen to get us a couple of Cokes.

He was not on the couch when I got back. I felt terrific panic and was about to rush to his room when I saw him. He was standing in front of the hall mirror and his mouth was open in a scream but no sound was coming out of it. Before I got to him his fists crashed against the glass and it splintered and he was trying to pry the pieces out and I fought him down. He stopped struggling and went completely limp and I thought he had fainted. His eyes were rolled back in his head, only the whites showing, and his mouth was still open in that horrible way as if he was actually screaming but the sounds were locked inside of him. And it wasn't his violence that scared me. He couldn't help that. It didn't really belong to him. The silence is what scared me. That silence did belong to him and it was his real enemy.

He had slumped in a heap against the wall and he was back in that hugging position, motionless, all tangled up in himself. And he looked more terrified than ever. I was no help to him anymore. The circles, or whatever he was scared of, had moved inside of him, and I could not go after them to destroy them.

I called our doctor. The answering service promised to find him right away and I asked for an ambulance too. It felt terrible, asking some stranger to take Kevin away but I was so certain by then that I couldn't do anything for him and that he was in great danger.

When I got back to him he was in exactly the same position. The only thing about him that was alive was his breathing and the occasional batting of his eyelids. I just sat on the floor with him until they came. The two ambulance attendants lifted him up, still in that round ball-like position. I rode inside the ambulance looking at his pale face. He looked peaceful because the doctor had given him a shot. I couldn't talk to the doctor because I was crying. All I told him was that Kevin had taken LSD and all I heard him say was that he was taking him to the best specialist he knew.

I didn't get to go inside Sweetmountain. The last I saw of Kevin was the attendants taking him up the steps of this big house that didn't look like a hospital. Back home the doctor gave me something to make me sleep, but I woke up again when I heard mom and dad.

God, I'm tired. I am going to sleep without reading this over to see if it makes sense.

SUNDAY, JUNE 18

We drove to the hospital right after the ten o'clock Mass. I promised God that I would never bug Him for anything if only He would make Kevin all right and we could bring him home with us.

Earlier this morning dad called our doctor and he told him that it might be some time before Kevin could leave Sweetmountain. But he also said that there is a chance that he will be perfectly all right once the LSD wears off. And all I'm hoping for is that chance.

In the car we barely talk. Whenever mom or dad say anything it's full of guilt. If they hadn't read my notebook they wouldn't feel so rotten. I blame myself for that too and by the time we drive into the hospital grounds I feel responsible for the whole damn world being rotten.

"What kind of a phony name is that," I say to dad pointing to the sign SWEETMOUNTAIN. "Let's get Kevin out of here right away. It's probably a lousy place with lousy doctors and lousy . . ."

"It's a very good hospital," dad says.

"It has Doctor Given on the staff," mom says. "So what?" I say.

"He's been researching LSD," dad says, and mom adds, "He is supposed to know more about it than anyone else in the country."

"Damn it! Kevin needs us!" I shout at them.

"Kevin needs help," dad says. And then, after a moment he adds, "He still has us, but he needs more than that now."

I wish the place would look worse than it does. If it did it would be easier for me to convince them that we have to get Kevin out of there. But the grounds and the buildings look like some kind of an estate, for God's sakes. It's a mental hospital and you'd expect there would be iron bars across the windows but there aren't, and there aren't any nuts running around shouting. As a matter of fact it's so empty we don't see a soul before we go inside through an unlocked front door. We're actually lost for a moment until we see a dame in a nurse's uniform and dad asks her where we can find this Doctor Given. She takes us to his office and it smells of pipe tobacco and is full of heavy furniture and thick books.

He is seated behind a desk writing something and he doesn't even raise his head when we come in. I mean it takes him about five minutes to notice us. And when he does he doesn't bother to be polite or anything. I really dislike him from the start.

"I want to find out as much as I can from you," he says and looks at each one of us separately. "Let's begin with you." And he points at me with his pipe. "What do you know about your brother?"

"You mean about him and LSD?" I ask him, trying not to sound annoyed. And man, does he annoy the hell out of me!

"No, about him as a human being," he says. I really hate the guy. The way he speaks and acts it's as if he wanted to let us know that we're interfering with his life or something.

"How is he? How is Kevin?" Mom asks. I see how worried she looks so I sort of shout at the guy: "Yeah, how about telling us how he is?"

"He hasn't come out of it yet," he says and then just looks at me as if waiting for me to answer.

"What do you mean he hasn't come out of it?" I say. "Does he still think the circles are choking him?"

"That seems to be his delusion, yes," he says and again he stares at me. I can't figure this guy. How can a doctor be so damn inhuman?

"What would you like him to tell you?" It's dad who says that. "Jim, please cooperate with Doctor Given."

"How the hell can I do that?" I sort of shout. "Let him ask me an intelligent question and I will."

"I asked you one," the guy says. Just like that, not even repeating it or anything. And he's just sitting there staring at me and drawing on that stinking pipe of his. If that's the way he wants to play it, O.K.

"I think Kevin is the greatest person I've ever known," I say and then, for good measure I add: "He's probably the greatest you'll ever know."

He's writing something down and doesn't look up when he asks me another stupid question.

"Is that all?"

"What do you mean is that all?" I almost shout at him. "Does he know you feel about him that way?"

"Sure he does!"

All I can think of is that this guy is no good for Kevin. He's an arrogant, stupid jerk.

"All right," he says, turning to mom, "what are your feelings about your son?"

"We all love him," mom says. "Kevin has always been a very special child, a very marvelous boy. We're all proud of him and—"

"Can you speak for yourself," the guy says, writing something down and not looking up at her, "rather than identifying with the family?"

"But we are a family," mom says.

"Yes, but you must have your own personal feelings about your son, what he means just to you?" He has taken the pipe out of his mouth and points it, like a gun, at mom. She looks uneasy, but she isn't like me. She won't get mad at him.

"I always had great hopes for Kevin." She says it as if it was something she was ashamed of admitting. "I've always . . . admired him." She laughs a sort of a timid laugh. "I know it's a strange thing to say, but I always did admire him, even when he was a small child. He was so . . . so superior to other children. I mean he was always brighter and . . ."

She is having difficulty in going on and I know she wants to cry but is too proud to do it in front of this jerk. Instead of being kind and gentle with her, he turns to dad:

"How about you?" he asks.

"We all feel the same way about Kevin," dad says. "He's someone very special in our lives."

"Where does he go to school?" the guy asks.

"University of Chicago," dad says.

"Whose decision was that, to send him there"?

"His."

"When did he decide to leave home?"

"At the end of his senior year," mom says. "He had applied to several colleges. What were they, dear, Columbia and NYU and . . ."

"Queens and CCNY," dad adds.

I don't see what all that information has to do with what is wrong with Kevin and I am about to say so but the guy is nodding his head and chewing on his pipe stem and saying:

"Interesting, interesting. And was he accepted at all of those colleges?"

"Yes," dad says. "He even had a scholarship at two of them . . ."

The guy gets up as if he was finished with us or something.

"Can we see him now?" mom asks. I look at her and she looks real small and timid and frightened.

"I'm afraid not," the guy says. Just like that. No explanations, no nothing. He is showing us to the door and saying, "We'll be in touch with you."

And we're leaving, like a bunch of sheep! By the time we reach the car I'm boiling mad. Not only at the doctor but at mom and dad. But mostly at that jackass Doctor Given.

"Who the hell does this jerk think he is?" I shout to dad. "Let's get back in there and get Kevin out."

"We can't do that," dad says.

"Why the hell not?" I yell. "What the hell's stopping us?" I don't usually swear like that in front of my parents but there is nothing usual about today and what's happening.

"Doctor Given must know best," mom says.

"I forgot to give Doctor Given your notebook." Dad had reached into the back seat of the car and is holding it now in his hand.

"Oh, no you don't!" I shout, grabbing for it. "I wouldn't give that creep the time of day."

But dad is holding on to it. "He needs it," he says. "It might help Kevin."

"I won't let him have it!" I say, trying again to take the notebook from him.

"Please, Jimmy." Mom is almost crying. And dad looks miserable too. "We have to give it to him," he says and walks away.

I get into the car and slam the door. For this guy to read what I've written is about the worst thing I can think of. I'm sure that all that guy is after is messing up all our lives. He'll poke around that notebook, misunderstanding everything, and he'll look at us as if we were some kind of rats in his lab. I wish I had never seen him! And I wish dad had guts like his father. I bet anything in the world that granddad wouldn't let Kevin be kept in a place that has such a jerk for a doctor.

On the way home I don't talk to them at all. They're pretty quiet at first and then they both begin to talk, interrupting each other, each one saying that it's not the other one's fault. I listen for a while and then I can't stand it anymore.

"What the hell are you talking about?" I shout at them. "It's the fault of that junk he took. That's all! All we ever did was love him. Nobody's guilty of anything!"

I don't know much about those people, analysts and psychiatrists and things, but if I were mom and dad I wouldn't let anyone fool around with Kevin, especially not that Doctor Given. He could change Kevin. He could turn him against us. I mean the way he questioned us, he wasn't impressed by the fact that we love Kevin and think he is the most special thing in our lives. He actually seemed to disapprove of that!

MONDAY, JUNE 19

They called from Sweetmountain. The effects of LSD have worn off, but we can't see him! We probably won't be able to see him for several weeks.

100

It wasn't even Doctor Given who called, but some assistant or secretary. Mom talked to them and then she called dad to tell him what they said and I listened on the extension. She sounded relieved, as if it was good news!

I had a horrible fight with her over that and I've never really fought with her before. I called her stupid and everything and I stormed out of the house. I was going to get drunk. I even went to a bar but they asked me for my ID and I left. I was going to go to the Wigwam but what would have been the use? I couldn't face anybody I knew, so I just walked for about five hours, getting wet because it's raining. In fact, It's been raining for days.

It wasn't until I was back in my room that I finally figured out what I ought to do. I ought to get Kevin out of that place! I don't care what mom and dad say or think, that's about the worst place for him. He'd be better off in the East Village with the hippies than with that madman Given.

WEDNESDAY, JUNE 21

I couldn't do it yesterday or today so it will have to be tomorrow. Mom has to go to an afternoon meeting of her charity thing. I'm going to take the Long Island Railroad to Sweetmountain. I plan to sneak into Given's office first and take the notebook away. Then I'm going to find Kevin. I know he must be dying to get out. He'd know best how we could do that.

I can't even say a civil word to either mom or dad anymore. Something happened to them. They've been brainwashed, I think. They don't understand that the most important thing for us to do is get Kevin back home. They think that Kevin should stay on there until Given discharges him. Yeah, that will be the day that Kevin promises to disown us.

I am not just imagining that that guy is all evil. Look at what he's done to us! To me! I am beginning to hate mom and dad. He is responsible for that! And I hate everybody else, including the kids I know. I went to the Wigwam and I saw my old friends for the first time since school ended and they're a bunch of idiots. I can thank Given for that too!

Well, tomorrow everything will be all right. Tomorrow I'm getting Kevin out!

THURSDAY, JUNE 22

I decided against going to Sweetmountain today. Instead I'm going to go to the East Village to find that girl. I had this idea that I might have to take Kevin somewhere other than our house. With mom and dad acting the way they do our house wouldn't be any better than that lousy hospital. Besides, a lot of kids when they have problems go to the East Village. It's not only for drugs and things, it's to get away from home. People don't bug you there.

Anyway, I want to talk to that girl and find things out, things like how you go about finding a cheap place to live. Kevin and I might just do that. Or we might take mom's car and drive to Canada or California. Just the two of us. I decided that I could actually take care of him if he wasn't all that well yet. It doesn't mean that I stopped blaming myself for what happened. It's just that both of us know better now. I'm sure he wouldn't want to try that junk again. Maybe he won't even want to touch grass either. But that didn't seem to affect him like it did me. So if he wants to smoke it sometimes, I'd let him.

Anyway I'm going to ask that girl a whole bunch of questions. She must have known people who freaked out on acid and she'd tell me what it does and for how long. I'm sure she knows a hell of a lot more about this stuff than Given. And she seemed to have a lot of common sense. She'd tell me if it would be all right for Kevin to live in the East Village with the drug scene the way it is. I figure she isn't on anything like grass or acid and for a good reason, and she'd know if you can live there without using that junk.

On the subway I didn't even want to ride the front car. Once Kevin and I are together we'll do it again. On the way over I kept thinking how great it would be, just the two of us, living together someplace. We could do all the things we used to do when we were kids.

The way I figure it you don't have to grow up in everything. I mean if you find something really great to do, why would you want to change it, just because somebody might think it was childish? Like the movie games we used to play. I wouldn't mind playing them with Kevin when we're both in our eighties. And I bet that jackass Given would try to change that! He'd probably think it wasn't good for Kevin or something. I just bet he would.

I changed subways at 59th and Lexington and took a local to Astor Place. And then I walked east. I couldn't remember whether it was on 10th or 9th Street, that pad, or the number either, but I was sure I'd recognize the cruddy building if I saw it. But as I kept walking I got depressed. The whole neighborhood depressed me. I mean it really looked shoddy, even worse than before, and the rain didn't help. It was drizzling and I was pretty wet, my hair and my shirt and my pants too. As a matter of fact I almost didn't want to go on. I began to think it was a pretty stupid idea my coming. I mean Kevin told me how he felt about hippies, how he couldn't live among them. So I was about to turn back when I see this guy with the broken tooth, the one who took us to the pad. He recognizes me and smiles and says hello.

"How was your brother's trip?" he asks me.

"He's in a hospital," I say and then I tell him how bad it was and how he saw those circles and how he almost killed himself trying to fight them and the guy is listening and nodding and when I stop he says: "Yeah, man, it happens like that sometimes. I'm sorry your brother freaked out. Has he come out of it yet?"

"Yes," I tell him.

"Then he'll be O.K.," he says. "It's only those guys who don't come out for a while that have it tough."

I want to ask him about what happens to them but I don't. Instead I ask him about the girl, where I can find her.

"I don't know her name. She was taking a bath in your pad . . ."

"Yeah, that was Marcia. She's helping out at the Diggers' Free Store," he says.

"Where is that?" I ask.

"Down the street," he says. "I have to go that way myself. I'll show you."

He is still walking funny in that swinging way he has, and I have trouble keeping up with him without actually trotting. I'm afraid that he will ask me what I want with the girl but he doesn't. He mutters something about tough luck and I guess he is talking about Kevin. I really had a chance to ask him all those questions from before but I was too worried about what I was going to say to Marcia. Maybe I won't talk to her at all, I tell myself. Maybe I'll just say hello and look over the place she's working. The more I think about it, the stupider the idea of coming and living in the East Village seems to me.

"It's down the steps," he says. "She's in there." We're in front of a dump of a store and if he wasn't standing beside me, waiting for me to go in, I wouldn't have. But he's still there, so I go down the steps almost falling over some books. It's a real rutty-looking place. There are a couple of cartons sitting around with things hanging out of them like cruddy dresses. And against the wall, on a long hanger, are more sad-looking clothes, jackets and coats and dresses and suits and sweaters. As far as I could see there was nothing in that whole place worth having, except maybe for half a motorcycle that was propped up against the wall.

I didn't see her right away. When I did I pretended that I hadn't. She was sitting on top of a bunch of cartons. She looked very different. For one thing she was dressed in a long ratty sweater and jeans, and her hair was down all over her face. It didn't look as great as when she wore it piled up. Now it just looked dirty and stringy. All of a sudden I didn't really want to talk to her anymore, not in that cruddy place. I know that sounds strange and everything, because I had been so crazy about her, wanting her to come and live at our house. But it wasn't the same anymore. Maybe because I am such a snob, but this place depressed me so much I felt like crying.

A couple of hippies were trying some shirts on and a Negro lady was going through those miserable-looking clothes while her kids were spilling things out of one of the boxes. I didn't know what I should do. I didn't want to leave because I was afraid of bumping into the guy with the missing tooth again. But I also didn't want to waste the whole trip. I had really come to help Kevin. So after standing around pretending to look over some books, and hoping she'd speak to me first, I finally went up to her and said hi.

"Hi," she says and I know she doesn't recognize me. She's bending over one of her boots. "They're killing me," she says, pointing. "They're full of holes or something. They feel so rough on the inside."

The boots look pretty new to me and I'm about to say that they might be too small for her when she takes them off and turns them over and I can see that the soles are all ragged. I mean they hardly have any soles. They look as if whoever made them didn't bother to finish them.

"You should have them soled," I say.

"Groovy. How do I do that?" she asks and looks at me.

"Take them to a shoemaker," I say.

"That would take bread," she says. She's holding on to those miserable boots and I look down at her bare feet and they aren't too clean. Actually they're filthy. "Can't I fix them myself?" she asks.

Her voice is not so much soft as lazy-sounding. It

106

really takes her a long time to speak, and when she does, to get it all out.

"Sure, you could fix them," I say. "You can fix them by gluing a piece of inner tube to the soles." Once we went to Haiti during Easter and I saw people walking around with shoes made of the outer part of a tire, the thick part, but that wouldn't look too good so that's why I said inner tube. It's thinner but it would protect her feet, I figure.

"Groovy," she says and begins to put the boots back on her feet and makes sort of moaning sounds while she's doing it. They look much too small for her. I don't know why I said the next thing. Maybe I felt real sorry for her.

"Did you run away from home?" I ask her.

"I walked away. I didn't run away," she says and smiles at me. "Don't mind me," she says very slowly. "I'm kind of up. I should be down by now, but I am not. But by . . . hey, what time is it?"

I look at my watch. "It's half past three, almost," I tell her.

"By five I ought to come down."

I didn't really know what she was talking about, if she meant coming down from those cartons or coming down from some drug.

"Or maybe I won't," she says. I have the feeling that she is talking more to herself than to me. "Maybe from now on I'll always stay up. Forever." She giggled and said "groovy" a couple of times.

"Why did you leave home?" I ask her, wanting to get back to more practical things. I hated the way she seemed, all confused and so relaxed she was almost falling apart at the seams. She didn't answer but she kept looking at me and so I repeated the question again.

"Mother," she says and starts looking around the store, over my head.

"Did she bug you?"

"Man, did she bug me." She says it slowly and then laughs very softly but there is no expression in her eyes. That really bothered me, that lack of anything in her eyes. I figure that she has forgotten what we were talking about but then she says, "Mother is a career woman." But the way she says it I don't know if she's bragging about it or condemning her mother for it.

"Hey, look, aren't they groovy?"

She is pointing to the kids who by now have emptied one of the boxes all over the floor. A couple of white kids are there too, three or four years old, sort of miniature hippies, with beads and long dirty hair. All the kids are laughing like crazy and throwing things at each other.

"Hey, hey, they're groovy," the girl says, but her eyes aren't laughing. They don't change at all. And her face stays the same, pale and tired-looking. I even think that she is sick, with maybe tuberculosis or something awful like that.

"Do you work here, for money I mean?" I ask her. I figure she should stop the kids from messing up the place, but also I want to know if she is starving or anything and I wish I'd brought some money along to give her.

"No, I come in here when I feel like it," she says. "Nobody works here for money. We give things away." She looks at me and there is now a flicker of life in her eyes. Or maybe it's pride. "We don't ever sell anything here. We just give things away."

I am tempted to say that it would be pretty tough to sell any of that junk, but I don't.

"I really dig kids," she says, looking towards the mess in the middle of the store. "Kids and cats. I used to have five cats once." Then she gets this thoughtful look on her face. "One day," she says real slowly, "I'll get my own pad and I'll take kids in. Little kids. Maybe even babies. Yes, babies nobody wants. I'll advertise." She giggles softly to herself. "Kids can't read," she says, "so I won't advertise. They'll find me somehow. See, I'll have this large pad, with lots of sun coming in, and white walls and some flowers or plants inside, and it will be all green and white and shadows. And the kids will come to live with me. I'll give a kitten to each kid, for their very own. The kittens won't have any names until the kids give them names. And we'll all dig it there. We'll be grooving it all day . . ."

She stops talking but I think she is still thinking about how it will be, except she doesn't want to tell me anymore. Maybe she knows I don't believe it will really ever happen. Maybe she understands that much. And all I can hope for is that she believes in it. If only she really believes her dream then I would not have to feel sorry for her.

But I can't help it. Nothing really wonderful is going to happen to her, I keep thinking. And again I feel like asking her to come and live with us, but I can't do it because she'd know I'd be asking out of pity now.

God, I was almost going out of my mind trying to stop feeling sorry for her. I pity the way she sits and the way her boots are, and the way her voice sounds. I pity the pad she lives in and that store she works in and the whole way she lives. The only thing I don't pity about her is that dream of a sunny place with kids' and cats in it. I love her dream, even though I don't believe it. I really love *her* for having that dream.

"Good-bye," I say.

"Aren't you grooving around here?" she asks.

"No," I say. "I don't know how to groove."

It sounded stupid and square and silly but that's how it is and I wanted her to know it.

FRIDAY, JUNE 23

I hitchhiked to Sweetmountain. The guy who gave me a lift took me all the way there and it was out of his way. He was really nice, a salesman. I swear he could have been Willy Loman. That's my favorite play, "Death of a Salesman," I mean. And the guy who gave me the lift never heard of it. I mean I did ask him whether he's seen it on television and he said no.

"I'm on the road all the time," he said. "When I check into a motel that has a TV I'm usually too tired to watch it."

That's how Willy Loman would be.

"What do you sell?" I asked him.

"Shoes," he said. "Ladies', men's, and children's shoes."

That's about the most success-proof thing he could be in. I mean with all the shoe stores around why would anyone want to buy shoes from him?

"How is business?" I asked him.

"Not so good," he said.

He wasn't really old, maybe sixty at the most, but boy, do I feel for the guy. I mean it must be terrible to be a traveling salesman anyway, but when business is bad it must be hell. I wish I had taken some money with me so I could buy a pair off him and I told him so. He handed me this catalog and I looked through it and there were the most miserable shoes I've ever seen. I mean real awful. The catalog doesn't even call them shoes. It calls them "footwear." And they're real expensive, like $17.95. I felt like telling the guy that he's wasting his time, that nobody in their right mind would buy expensive shoes that looked like that, but I didn't say anything because that might have hurt his feelings. So we just rode not saying much, and I kept leafing through that miserable catalog, muttering things like "hmm, interesting color," and stuff like that. "I've got a nice line of merchandise," he says. "Those are sharp-looking." He stabs his finger at a page that has all those pointy shoes for men, the two-tone jobs, some even with stuff on them that looks like the cane they have on furniture. I mean the kind of things they might have worn in the thirties, in the gangster movies, but even gangsters today wouldn't be caught dead in them.

"Yeah," I say. "Are those your hot items?"

"They move fast in Vermont and Maine," he says.

"What do you do, cover New England?"

"That's my territory," he says. "It's been mine for thirty-six years."

It's too incredible that he never heard of Willy Loman! All of a sudden I thought about that lady in the store in the East Village, the tweedy type who doesn't bother with life changing, and I figure that she and this guy would make a nice pair, so I ask him if he's married.

"I'm a widower," he says. "My wife passed on three years ago."

"Do you have any children?"

"They're grown," he says. He didn't have to say any more. I just know his kids don't even bother seeing him. I just know they don't give a damn about their old man. I bet that he'd like to be around his grand-children but they probably only invite him over once a year on Thanksgiving or something. I mean I was sitting in his car, looking out of the window, getting real mad at his lousy kids and I don't even know them, for God's sakes!

We were in front of the gate to Sweetmountain before I knew it and so I tried to tell him about that lady in the store.

"She's a very nice lady," I said. "If you're around Second Avenue and 8th Street . . ."

"What's her name?" he asked.

"I don't know," I said, feeling real dumb. "She has this storefront office sort of thing, on the west side of the avenue."

He didn't seem interested enough for me to continue. "Good luck," I said to him. "And thanks for the lift."

"We should have stopped for coffee or a Coke," he said and sounded sorry to be leaving me. That really got me. I mean I practically had tears in my eyes as I walked away from him.

I was still thinking of the guy as I walked up the steps. I mean I wasn't going to do that. I was going to sneak in, sort of look around the grounds to see how I could get Kevin to escape without being noticed. But it was too late. The same nurse who took us to Doctor Given's office was looking down at me and saying hello. I felt like an absolute fool. There were about half a dozen people on the porch, sitting on chairs and playing chess or cards or something and this nurse was staring at me and I didn't know what to tell her. I wasn't supposed to be there, for God's sakes.

"Would you like to see Doctor Given?" she is asking me.

"No," I tell her. "I want to see my brother."

"Well, we'd best see Doctor Given first."

I couldn't give her an argument in front of all those patients so I follow her, feeling like a real jackass.

He's behind his desk like the last time I saw him, except his chair is turned toward the window and all I can see of him is the top of his head and the smoke that comes from his pipe. I wait for him to turn around but when he speaks his back is still to me.

"You can't see your brother," he says.

"Why not?" I didn't mean to shout but I did.

"Because he doesn't want to see you."

"You're lying!"

Very slowly he brings his chair around and faces me and he's looking straight at me and I tell him again that he's lying, this time more quietly so that he knows I mean it. I hate him so much I actually can't stand the sight of him.

He points his pipe toward the phone on his desk.

"Pick it up and dial 10. That's his room. Ask him yourself if he wants to see you."

I grab the phone and the receiver drops from my hands and hits his desk with a bang. All I know is that I don't believe him. In a minute I'll hear Kevin tell me that he wants to see me.

"Hello." It's him.

"I came to see you," I say. "I'm downstairs. Are you coming down or should I go up?"

He doesn't say anything for a moment and when he speaks I can barely hear him.

"I don't want to see you," he says.

"They've brainwashed you!" I'm shouting into the phone. "I came to get you out!"

"I want to stay here," he says. "I've got to find out all kinds of things. I can't see you until I do."

He says he's sorry but it would be best for him if he didn't see me for a while.

"How about me?" I shout.

"I'm the one who is sick," he says. "Please understand—"

I slam the receiver down then and turn to run out of the office, and behind me I hear Doctor Given say: "Do you want your notebook?"

I didn't answer him and ran out of there, down the hall and down the steps and across the driveway, through the gates and down the street. All I know is that Kevin doesn't care anymore. All those years I loved someone who never gave a damn for me.

MONDAY, AUGUST 7

Kevin called this morning. He talked to mom and then asked to talk to me. I told her to tell him that I wasn't in. I said it loud enough for him to hear. She tried to argue with me so I said that I didn't want to talk to him and walked out of the room.

He called again this afternoon and I answered the

phone because I thought it was one of the guys I was supposed to play tennis with.

"Could you come over tomorrow?" he says. "I want to see you."

I'm about to hang up on him but I don't.

"Why?" I ask. "Why do you want to see me?"

"I'm well enough to talk to you now."

Again I almost hang up on him. I mean it's been so many weeks and he never wrote me or called me or anything.

"Please come tomorrow," he says.

I hate myself for crying and I don't want him to know that I am, so I say O.K. just so I can get off the phone. And then I hang up and start to think. But I can't make anything out.

Ever since I came back from that place I've tried not to think about him and whenever mom and dad talk about him I leave the room. It isn't that I hate him. That would even be all right, I mean it would help, feeling hate for him. But I don't hate him. All I wanted to do was forget about him. I tore up all the pictures I had of him and the couple of letters he sent me from Chicago. I haven't even watched any old movies on television so I wouldn't be reminded of him. But I've been feeling worse and worse every day. If only he hadn't said that, about not wanting to see me. He could have told it to me in person. In person I could have taken anything from him. But he did it on the phone. He didn't even bother to see me to tell me he didn't want to see me.

Boy, I just read the above. How dumb can I be? I really didn't have a good reason for wanting to forget Kevin. I realize now that all those weeks I was cheating myself. I thought that something complicated, something very hard to understand, had happened between me and Kevin. But it's all been so simple. I had my feelings hurt, for Christ's sakes! That's all! My cruddy feelings were hurt! And all this time he was sick, trying to get better. Really working at it. God, how dumb can I be!

Anyway, tomorrow I'll see him. *He wants to see me!*

TUESDAY, AUGUST 8

In the car, on the way over to Sweetmountain, I told mom that it was very important to me to see Kevin alone. She said she understood and didn't ask any dumb questions.

"I'll wait in the car while you see him first," she said. But it didn't work out that way. He was waiting for us, sitting on the porch steps. He ran over to the car even before it stopped. He yanked the door open and got mom out and hugged her and kissed her before he even glanced at me.

"Doctor Given wants to see you," he said to her. "While you do that I'll talk to Jimmy." And then, finally, he looked at me. His eyes were a little shiny but they were not strange anymore. And he was smiling.

"Hi," he said. "How've you been?"

"O.K.," I said. I watched mom climb up the steps because I didn't dare stare at him. There was something new about him. I didn't trust it. I was afraid of it.

"Let's walk," he said.

We went down the long curving driveway without speaking, and came to the gate. "Don't they ever lock this thing?" I asked him, just to say something.

"I don't really know," he said. He was thinking hard, really concentrating on something. We turned right and walked on the sidewalk, past some houses with lawns sloping down toward the street. Suddenly he laughs and points to his right.

"Hey, look at that!"

I look to where he is pointing and there, on the lawn, is a large sign: KEEP OFF THE GRASS.

"That's pretty good advice," I say.

"Sure it's good advice," he says. "It should be given by the right people, though, not the same ones who dump grass with acid and speed."

"It's all the same junk," I say.

"You're crazy if you think that!" He had raised his voice but he was smiling. "Doctor Given—"

"He's a jackass," I say.

"To you, maybe. He just happens to know more about all that stuff than anyone else, that's all. He thinks that grass can hurt you only when you get dependent on it. It dulls your mind like alcohol does but it can't make you freak out. The thing is, with grass, you get dependent on it. You use it when you've got problems and pretty soon you begin to think that you've got something going for you. But you've got nothing. It doesn't change a thing. All it does is make you cheat yourself. If it could cure you of your hang-ups it would be great, but it doesn't. It makes you think your hang-ups are not important. So you don't do anything about them. But they're still with you and getting worse all the time."

"Will you ever take it? Will you ever smoke grass?"

"I don't intend to. I'm going to try to make it with what I've got going for me."

I want to ask him about LSD, but he keeps on talking. "Grass might be O.K. for some people who aren't in a hurry, who want to goof off for a while longer. But once you're impatient to get on with life, all it can do for you is slow you down. And I'm in a hurry now. I haven't got the time. I could be drafted if I don't do well at college this year. God, I've wasted so much time!"

He jumps up and touches a branch that's about ten feet off the ground. He doesn't say anything for a moment, not until after he kicks a stone out of the way.

"All those creeps who dump acid with grass! Man, acid can maim you for life! It can do worse than that! It can keep you in a nut house forever! It just isn't even close to grass, for God's sakes! And speed! That stuff is a real killer, and that's no propaganda. You get on speed and you last no more than two years. You're dead! But before you die you can kill someone. It's far worse even than heroin."

"What about you? What made you take acid?" I felt like a jerk, asking him that. I realized all of a sudden that I should have known. What the hell was I doing all those years, not knowing him?

"I got myself real screwed-up. I used a hell of a lot of ingenuity and imagination in getting myself screwed-up. I don't know everything yet. Maybe I'll never know anything, but at least I'm making a start." He laughs and looks at me. "Hey, do you remember my not wanting to tell you something that happened when I was a real small kid?"

I nod my head and he's shaking his.

"It wasn't anything important. But I thought it was. I thought what happened was about the most important thing . . ."

He lifts himself up and sits on a fieldstone wall and motions me to sit beside him. I can't make it alone so he gives me a hand and pulls me up.

"You were about two, I guess," he says. "Anyway, one night I heard mom and dad have this awful argument. You know how they are, so quiet and polite, but they were really yelling at each other." He laughs. "You were always a sound sleeper. I used to worry about that, about you sleeping like a rock. Anyway, they woke me up and at first I didn't know what was happening and I got scared and hid under the blanket. But the blanket didn't keep their voices out so I began to cry and call for them but they couldn't hear me. I got out of bed and ran to their room. I was going to beg them to stop. But before I got to their bedroom I heard mom say that if it hadn't been for me and you she would have left dad a long time ago. And then dad said the same thing, that if it hadn't been for us, especially for me, he would have left her. And then they quieted down and began to speak in normal voices saying how great I was and how it would ruin my life if they got divorced. They also said that to you it wouldn't matter so much because you were so little, but it would kill me. I just stood there listening to them and crying all over my pajamas. And before I went back to sleep that night I promised myself that I would always be a good boy." He stops talking then and reaches up over his head and gets an apple. It's a lousy one, bumpy and not ripe yet, so he reaches for a better one and hands it to me and starts eating the lousy one himself. We munch on them, making faces and spitting out the skins. It's really too early for apples.

"So what happened?" I ask him. "How did that screw things up for you?"

"Well, all those years I must have been thinking that it was up to me to keep the family together. Doctor Given says—"

"How can you believe anything that creep says?" I shout at him. He looks at me surprised.

"I didn't even tell you what he said."

"I just don't trust the guy, that's all."

"Why don't you?" Kevin asks.

"I don't know. I just don't."

"Well, I do," Kevin says. "For one thing he never told me anything that I didn't know or sort of suspect. All he really does is throw a light and then I can see for myself . . ."

"What does he say? Does he say that we're one rotten family? Is that what he's trying to make you believe?"

"Of course not! Where the hell did you get that idea?"

"I know what he's up to!"

"You don't understand . . ."

"I do too understand! He probably made you believe that your family isn't worth saving!"

"He made me believe it's not in any danger!"

"Without you it is!" I don't know why I said that. And now I tried to cover it up. "He's changed you."

"I hope he's helping me to change."

"There was nothing wrong with you! You were O.K. the way you were."

He looked at me hard then.

"I am not going to be as I was." He said it very slowly and I looked away from him because I couldn't stand it, him staring at me as if he wanted to be sure that I was going to accept that. "I will never be as I was."

"But I want you—"

"Listen! You have to understand!" He's shaking me by the shoulders now and we both slide off the wall and land on our feet. He hasn't let go of me and he keeps looking at me hard and I can't look away anymore. "I will love you more, not less. Don't you see? When you're all screwed-up you can't love anybody properly." He lets go of me and when he speaks again it's much more quietly. "I'm just making a beginning, but I'm making it! And I can't be the same. All those years . . ."

"They were wonderful years," I shout at him. "There was nothing wrong with those years!" I keep thinking that they want to even take the past away from me, him and that Doctor Given. And I'm not going to let them!

"In many ways they were wonderful," he says, but I don't want to listen. If I were a kid I'd have put my hands over my ears. "But in many ways they were rotten. You never knew it, but I had to practically kill myself to keep up in school. When everyone was asleep I'd wake up to do more studying . . ."

"You were a genius! You never needed to study."

"I did. I had to work harder than any guys in my school."

"That's not true!"

"Yes it is. Don't you understand what I am trying to tell you? I tried to live up to everybody's idea of me! Kevin The Genius! But all along I was just an average kid pretending to be more . . ."

"You're not average! You're special!"

"I'm not! I'm nothing special. But I hope to be one day."

I began to run away from him. I couldn't listen to him. I can't stand it, him believing those lies about himself.

He tackles me from behind and we both fall down. I struggle with him, but he's stronger and gets hold of my hands and then he makes me get up.

"You've got to listen to me." He talks to me slowly, not angrily or loud. "You must understand! Mom and dad don't need to know, but you, you must know how it is with me. You destroyed the circles for me once and you must do that again. For both of us this time."

"There were no circles!"

"But there were! Maybe not the kind I saw, but they were real all the same. At first I made those circles myself. And later you and mom and dad helped. Don't you see, if you live up to something you are not, you live in prison! And that's what those circles were. Look, I don't want you to feel guilty about anyhing. You're not guilty and neither is mom or dad. I let you do it. So it's only my business, really. It's all been my mistakes."

I wasn't looking at him. He waited for me to say something, but I couldn't. I wanted to tell him that it was all a bunch of lies, dreamed up by that doctor, and I for one didn't believe them. But I didn't say anything and then he spoke again.

"I'm not a genius! I'm not special! I want to be who I can be and I need your help."

I tried to get loose but he was still holding on to my hands. "Let me go," I said.

"Not until you try to understand."

"I won't understand," I shouted at him. "I won't ever understand why you let that creep Given—"

"Damn it! He wasn't anywhere around when I freaked out! Don't you remember how I was? I must have been pretty screwed-up. And I could have stayed that way all my life! There is one boy back there"—he pointed towards the hospital—"who thinks he's on fire. He took the trip six months ago! Six months!"

"But you came out of it!"

"Only because I decided to grow up. And you're not going to hold me back. And do you know why you can't anymore?" He wasn't asking me. He was telling me. "It's because I no longer want to be held back!"

He let go of my hands then and I ran away from him. All I know is I was crying. And all I can understand is that he used to belong to me and he doesn't now. I've lost him. For good this time.

TUESDAY, SEPTEMBER 5

It's been one rotten summer. In a couple of days school starts. All I've done all summer long is sleep and eat. I didn't even read the books I was supposed to. I'd go to the Wigwam and just sit around listening to the guys talk cars and girls and crap like that and then I'd go home and take a nap. I didn't even play tennis more than a couple of times.

Kevin stayed on at Sweetmountain all summer. He didn't have to. He wanted to stay and got a job doing odd things around the place. He'd call mom and dad a couple of times a week and he wrote me one letter. I didn't even open it. I flushed it down the toilet.

He's coming back for a couple of days before he has to go to Chicago. I was thinking of moving out, maybe going off to some beach or something until he leaves. But then, as I was throwing some of my things into a suitcase I got to reading both my notebooks. And when I finished with them I changed my mind about going.

I don't even know if they've invented a word that would fit me. I mean I ran out on him when he needed me, and that's about the lousiest thing a human being can do.

The last thing he said to me was that he intended to grow up. When the hell will I ever do that? Growing up means changing, and I still hate that. And letting go is part of it too, and I wouldn't let him go. If there's any hope for me at all, I'll see it in the way I act when he gets here. The thing is I don't even know if he wants to talk to me or anything.

The real stupid thing was that he found me crying. I was sitting in my room bawling like a little kid. When he came in I wanted him to hug me and tell me to stop. He made a move toward me as if he wanted to do that, but then he didn't.

"We won't play movie games again," I said, rubbing my crummy tears away. I felt like an idiot because that's not what I meant to say. I was going to ask him to forgive me.

He reached to mess up my hair and I had thought that he'd never do that again.

"Sure we will," he said and then he did his Cody Jarrett bit: "How you doing, Parker? . . . You want some air? . . . I'll give you some air."

"I'll stop bugging you about being your Boswell," I said.

"Yeah, I hope you cut that out."

"I'll never write anything in my lousy notebooks again."

"Sure you will, but you won't have to write just about me."

"Then I looked up at him and he was standing there smiling. He's got long hair and sideburns and he's even begun to grow a moustache. I've got to get used to that but I think I'll like it. But what really makes me glad is he looks all right.

"You're really O.K.," I said. "And no creepy doctor needs to tell me that."

"So are you," he said. "So are you."

That's what *he* says. But I've got to prove it to myself that I can make it as a human being. On my own.

Today's
Hangups
and the
Generation
Gap

I'm really dragged but nothing gets me down

by Nat Hentoff
author of *Jazz Country*

Jeremy Wolf is a high school senior whose soul is torn between his responsibility to his country and his social existence. With wit and with rare understanding, this novel examines both sides of the generation gap.

"A taut, highly articulate exposition of today's hangups..."—*The Virginia Kirkus Service*

"...timely and important..."
—*The New York Times*

A LAUREL-LEAF BOOK   60c

For everyone who wants to understand the most crucial issue in America today . . .

BLACK STRUGGLE

A Short History of the Negro in America

The Black American's battle for freedom today has its roots in centuries of injustice. BLACK STRUGGLE recounts the history of the Negro from his early beginnings in Africa up to the headline-making events of today. While it is a chronicle of suffering the cruelties of slavery, the humiliation of segregation, and the imprisonment of urban ghettos, it is also a story of heroism: the daring exploits of black soldiers, the determination of slaves in revolt, the bravery of the underground railroad escapes and the courage of the civil rights martyrs.

A LAUREL-LEAF BOOK 75c

Three Collections of Essays and Stories on Youth, Alienation, and Discovery from Laurel-Leaf Library

EDGE OF AWARENESS   50c
edited by Ned E. Hoopes and Richard Peck

In this stimulating collection of 25 essays, statesmen, poets, anthropologists, critics, and scientists express their personal views on many subjects, from the problems of young people to the exploration of outer space.

POINT OF DEPARTURE   50c
edited by Robert S. Gold

Adolescence is a very trying, frequently anguished, period of life. This collection of 19 modern stories registers the full range of the youthful experience—the pain, the confusion, the excitement.

WHO AM I? Essays on the Alienated   75c
edited by Ned E. Hoopes

Twenty-seven renowned essays examine the dilemma of most youth today who are searching for a clearer picture of themselves, of their environment, of their society.